Shabine and Other Stories

Shabine
and Other Stories

HAZEL SIMMONS-McDONALD

The University of the West Indies Press
Jamaica • Barbados • Trinidad and Tobago

The University of the West Indies Press
7A Gibraltar Hall Road, Mona
Kingston 7, Jamaica
www.uwipress.com

ISBN: 978-976-640-905-0 (print)
978-976-640-907-4 (ePub)

Cover illustration and design by Kathleen McDonald
Book design by Robert Harris
Set in Scala 11/15.5 x 27

Previously published with some variations from the versions in this volume:
"The Flowering of Rosa", *Poui: The Cave Hill Literary Annual*, no. 1 (1999): 66–80.
"Shabine", *Poui: The Cave Hill Literary Annual*, no. 9 (2009): 118–22.
"Torn Pages", *Bim: Arts for the 21st Century* 5, no. 2 (2012): 48–61.
"Mirror", *Bim: Arts for the 21st Century* 6 (May 2013–May 2014): 95–101.
"Dear Departed". In *Thicker Than Water: New Writing from the Caribbean*, edited
    by Funso Aiyejina (Port of Spain: Peekash Press, 2018), 88–102.
"Tapestry", *Bim: Arts for the 21st Century* 9, no. 1 (2019): 53–62.
"Imogene", *Bim: Arts for the 21st Century* 10, no. 1 (2021): 39–49.

Printed in the United States of America

In memory of my sister, Alnita

Contents

Shabine

"Look me here. Yuh see me? Yuh stan up over deh watchin me. Yuh tink ah don see you? Look me here. I goin stan up under duh light for you to see me good. Come from duh shadow. Yuh want tuh see me? Well, come see me." Justine rose slowly from the old soap box on which she sat. Beneath the full, flared skirt of the red dress she wore most nights and which now cascaded from her hips, he could see the outline of firm buttocks, the slender shapeliness of her thighs. His heart beat faster, as much from excitement as from fear as to what she would do now that she had discovered him. They said she had a vicious temper. They said that her red hair which hung to her shoulders in a thick woolly tangle was testimony of that. They said she could do nothing about it even if she tried.

Once he had seen her burst through her front door, spitting profanities as she threw stones at the boys who had stood facing her house on the other side of the street, taunting her with the chant they had composed about her. They sang it first in Kwéyòl, the local lingo, and then in English.

Lò ek danjan, sa mwen ni	I have Gold I have Silver,
Tchwi ek diamans sa mwen pa ni	Copper and diamonds I don't have.
Ou wè mwen? Ou wè mwen?	You see me? You see me?
Vini bo mwen, vini bo mwen	Come kiss me, come kiss me,
Doudou jamette	Darling whore.

And they would press their palms to their mouths and make an exaggerated kissing sound.

Justine had two sons, whom she called Gold and Silver. Gold had the reddest crop of thick woolly curls and a shock of red bushy eyebrows that inevitably drew one's eyes to his freckled face, to the surprise of grey eyes and a vulnerable mouth that trembled as though he were always on the verge of tears. Silver was blond, sort of. His straight, close-cropped sun-bleached white hair stood out like spines from his head. He was fearless and would stand on his side of the street giving back taunt for taunt, repeating as a litany the only swear words he seemed to know. "Chou manma'w, yuh muddath athss," he would lisp through his large front-toothed gap. Gold would be there too, tugging at Silver's sleeve, trying to pull him away before the words erupted in a war of stone-throwing or before Justine appeared to end it with her own assault of words; the inevitable slap on Silver's rump; and the admonition "How many times I tell you not to interfere wif dese inyowan? How many times? Now you behavin' ignorant like dem. Go inside before I get vex an cut yuh tail."

"Dey trouble me first. An dey call you jamette. I don want dem to call you dat." And sometimes, Justine would hug Gold and Silver fiercely as if willing her embrace to erase the taunts, the slurs, the hurts that the residents of Riverside Road tossed her way.

She had lived in the two rooms that adjoined the large two-storeyed dwelling at No. 80 Riverside Road as long as she could remember. Her mother was Madame Cazaubon's maid and she had let her live in the servants' quarters with her little girl, Justine. Her mother died in Justine's late teens, from what everyone said was too much rum and grief because Misyé Cazaubon had never kept his promise to her to acknowledge Justine as his daughter and send her to Convent School. Instead, he allowed Madame Cazaubon to confine them to the two rooms in the yard and to treat Justine as though she were a servant too. That was the thing that seemed to annoy her mother the most. The times she seemed to get angry were when Madame Cazaubon would order Justine to fetch this or that.

"Pa palé ba li kon sa," her mother would say sharply. "Don' talk to her like dat. She not your maid, yuh hear?"

"Well! And who do you think you're talking to? This is my house, don't you forget that! And you'll never replace me here, slut!" Madame Cazaubon would swish her skirt and stalk off into the drawing room where she would sit in the high-backed chair next to the window, muttering under her breath until Mr Cazaubon got home. Then she would let loose a stream of invective in which she accused him of bringing shame, trials and tribulation into their home and making her the subject of gossip and ridicule among the neighbours on Riverside Road. Mr Cazaubon would gobble his food, go into his room and shut the door against the high-pitched whine of her voice.

Now Justine stood in the circle of light from the street lamp. One hand on her hip, the other twirling the thick woolly curls at the back of her neck. One strap of her dress fell off her shoulders and even in that faint light he could see the spray of chocolate freckles dotting her skin.

When he was much younger, his grandmother, who lived in the house next to the Cazaubons on Riverside Road and with whom he spent the long vacations, had warned him not to tease the Shabine, and if she found out that he had, she would make his bottom spit fire. That was a long time ago when he and Justine were both young. She couldn't have been more than a year or two older than he was. She had always fascinated him and, unknown to his grandmother, he would walk along the river wall to the Cazaubons' backyard and leave a paradise plum on the gate post. He would then climb the Julie mango tree in his grandmother's yard and, from the shelter of the thick spray of leaves, peek to see what Justine would do.

Soon enough, she would come to the fence, take the paradise plum, look directly at the mango tree, pretend that she didn't see anyone, seem bewildered, slowly unwrap the paper, place the paradise plum on the tip of her tongue and slowly curl it back into her mouth. He would sit motionless on his perch, watching this ritual of unwrapping and savouring and hold in his breath until she went into the house.

Years later, when he was in his final year at university, he spent the Easter holidays with his grandmother. On the very first day of his visit, she told him that even though he was a grown young man, he needed to listen to his betters who knew more than he thought they knew. She told him she knew all about his attraction to Justine and she warned him about enticing her. She told him Justine's mother had complained about his giving her paradise plums and putting ideas in her head. She said he had upset her and she wanted him to keep his distance.

Yet, one afternoon, while he sat quietly reading Shakespeare's *Anthony and Cleopatra* in the front room, preparing for his examination, he could hear the rush of the river rising, could smell the fragrance of paradise plums and he had the strongest urge to taste one. He crept out of the house and looked into her yard from the shelter of the Julie mango tree. He saw her leaning against the post, looking longingly at the river. Her hair seemed more exuberant, the chocolate freckles more stark against her pale skin. She seemed to sense that she was being observed and turned to stare, for what seemed to him to be an eternity, at the Julie mango tree. He could see that her stomach was swollen and full of Gold.

He had walked with leaden footsteps back to the house and had picked up his book, but the word "Shabine" filtered into every line of the play he was studying. "(Shabine) makes hungry where most she satisfies." He put down the book and sighed. He wondered why some of the people on the street called her "Shabine" with such contempt. He knew what the word meant literally. It defined her pale, reddish skin colour, the mass of coarsish red hair that resembled the wool of sheep, the grey eyes that looked directly at him only to glance away coyly, the chocolate freckles.

She wasn't like anyone else he knew. Not high coloured like Misyé Cazaubon, or white like the sailor he saw her mother usher surreptitiously into her house the last time he had visited; and certainly not Negro like her mother. She was a blend, a half-breed and to him more beautiful because of her difference. As the words "(Shabine) makes hungry" filtered into his thoughts again, he began to feel angry at the boys who taunted her by tossing the words "Shabine" and "jamette" at her every time she passed by. He felt angry at the distance between his grandmother's yard and hers, at the fact that no matter how often he traversed the wall space between their yards he would never be able to enter there. He thought about the chant the boys composed about her and imagined that, if things had been different, he could have been the diamond in her life. He felt angry at the waste of paradise plums he had left for her to pluck off the post in her yard; angry because he had been too timid; angry because he had avoided going over and eating them with her; angry at her mother for inviting the white stranger in.

Now a grown man in his mid-thirties, returning to arrange his grandmother's funeral, he stood watching her beneath the lamp. He wondered whether she too smelt the fragrance of paradise plums. She turned to face him directly where he stood in the shadow.

"Yuh see me?" she asked softly. "Yuh see me? Maybe yuh wan come kiss me too? Maybe?" She stared hard and long at him while his heart raced and the sound thundered so loudly in his ears he thought she must hear it. Then she turned, glanced at him over her shoulder, swept the mass of curls from her forehead and with a toss of her head walked back through the gate into the room in the yard and shut the door.

He thought that if things had been different, if there wasn't that stretch of wall between his house and hers, if in those early days they could somehow have claimed the afternoons by the river, savouring paradise plums together, that perhaps, just perhaps, there might have been plenty copper.

Mirror

Madeline sat facing the mirror. Strains of music from the gramophone were muffled from the buzzing in her ears.

It was my fault, wasn't it? Mine and George's. He betrayed you. He lied.

She stirred. The music had stopped and the needle was knocking against the capstan. It was early afternoon. Rain clouds were gathering. The metallic film, the tain in the mirror, was fading. The darkened space at the centre seemed to her like a tunnel leading to a pool, like the sea in the sheltered cove where she and Evon often went. A flash of lightning brightened the room. It occurred to her that she should find a cloth to cover the mirror, but her legs were leaden. She sat in a trance-like stupor, staring at it.

Why did you let him sweet talk you? What did he say to convince you Papa wasn't coming back? Eugenie and I knew George was a creep. He only wanted to have you. You let him hurt the man he called friend. George betrayed you and I've let Evon fool me. He got what he wanted and now he's gone. Everyone will laugh as they laughed when Papa left.

She shook her head. The buzzing persisted. It started to rain. She sat still, staring at the mirror. Eugenie entered.

"Doudou, you wake up? How you feelin? How duh head?" She stood behind the chair massaging Madeline's temples. "Pa kite kòw'u fòl pou séléwa sa-la. Don go mad for dat good fuh nuffin. Sleep shéwi; sleep, dear."

She closed her eyes; swallowed to still the buzzing in her ears. Eugenie stood behind the chair brushing her hair, singing the song her mother used to sing to her.

Look in the mirror what do you see?
One little girl pretty as can be
Who's pretty?
Maddieeeeee

Madeline would chime in at the last line, squealing her name in a high-pitched voice, collapsing with laughter. Eugenie's voice was soothing. She drifted off to sleep. Eugenie went to the gramophone. She put the stylus at the start of the record. Madeline had played it two nights before when she showed Evon how her mother and father used to dance. Through the mist of sleep Madeline heard the rhythm. She recalled the *clack clack* of her mother's heels striking the floor to the tempo as her father danced with her.

Her mother lived for the times when her father returned from a trip. He always brought gifts for her and her mother. He had brought the gramophone and records of popular merengue and love songs. One year he brought her mother dancing shoes. They were like ghillies, with decorative laces, high tops and solid heels. Her mother would wear a full, flared skirt that fell to her ankles and a broad belt with a gold buckle that accentuated her hips. They moved as one to the music, her left arm hugging his shoulders, her right circling his waist, her head thrown back, her eyes closed; a smile playing about her lips. His arms would be wrapped around her, holding her closely, his cheek against the side of her head, his eyes closed too, their hips moving in a quick up and down motion as they stepped to the beat, heels hitting the floor in unison, *clack-ti-clack*. She and Eugenie would watch them. Sometimes she fell asleep and Eugenie would put her to bed while her parents danced through the night.

One year her father stayed away an unusually long time. Her mother worried and seemed to wilt. Every day she dressed carefully in case he arrived unexpectedly. She would run to the window when she heard a car approaching. She would hurry to the mirror, check her looks; walk back to the window; look out; return to view herself in the mirror; sit in the chair, waiting. One day a car drove up to the house and George, her father's friend, walked in. Madeline couldn't hear what he said, but her mother had cried for days. After that George would stop by once in a while. Later, he would come every evening to sit and talk with her mother. Gradually, he would stay longer, leaving after Madeline had gone to bed.

One night Madeline heard the gramophone playing and the clack of heels on the floor. She rushed to the front room thinking her father was home. Instead, there was George, hair pomaded, two-tone shoes shining, his arms wrapped around her mother as her father's used to be. Her mother danced, but her arms hung limply by her side, and her eyes were open. The sight of her mother dancing with George disturbed Madeline. She started to cry. Eugenie calmed her.

"Don cry, shéwi. He goin jus now. I go mek him go." She took a broom, stuck it upside down in a shoe and put it behind the door. After a short while the music stopped. The front door closed. George left.

Several nights later she woke to the sound of voices in the front room. One was her father's. She got out of bed to go to him, but Eugenie met her at the door and led her back to bed, muttering, "Bon dyé senyè, lavyèj, édé nou – Good God, virgin, help us." She knew something bad must be happening to make Eugenie pray like that. She heard George's voice; a tussle; her mother's muffled scream. She had thought: It's *that* George. *He's a bad man.* She jumped out of bed, found a broom, stuck it upside down in a shoe behind the door as Eugenie had done when they had wanted to make George leave. She closed her eyes and wished him gone.

After a while she heard the front door close. She rushed out to greet her father, but there was George buttoning his shirt, glancing uneasily at her mother who was slumped in the armchair staring at her dishevelled reflection in the mirror. Eugenie was fussing over her, rubbing mustard on her forehead and temples to prevent a kwiz, Eugenie's Creole word for hysterics. Her mother didn't recover. Every day she would sit in the chair staring at the mirror. One day Madeline came home to find the chair empty and Eugenie crying because they had taken her mother away. Madeline was bereft. She felt an enormous guilt because she had put the broom in the shoe and made the wrong man go away.

She knew from the letters and money her father sent that he was in Latin America. His address was always different. When the letters stopped, she knew intuitively that her father had died. She grieved because her mother had left without saying goodbye and her father hadn't returned to see her.

You didn't even say goodbye and Papa never came back to see me. Now Evon has left. Everyone will laugh as they laughed when Papa left.

॰

Madeline reached out and touched his arm. "Don't go." He looked at her. He didn't answer.

"Evon, is this what you want?" He pursed his lips, looked away and bent down to tie his shoelaces.

"Stop dreaming, Madeline."

"What happened since last night?"

"Last night made me realize how wrong I am to keep up this charade."

Madeline raised one eyebrow quizzically. She looked at him as he stood up. He fixed his gaze on the wall behind her. There was nothing there except the mirror. She had meant to take it down when water had seeped through the roof and down the wall behind it. The rainy season had come and she hadn't had the roof repaired.

She had placed the mirror on the wall directly opposite the large one that sectioned the bureau into two parts. Her father had bought the bureau for her mother. It was made of mahogany. Two separate vines sprouted from the wood surface on each side, encircling the mirror and meeting at the top in a carved bunch of grapes tucked in a cluster of leaves. The rest of the bureau consisted of two sets of drawers on either side of the mirror. Her father had said the bureau was an antique that cost him a sum he wouldn't reveal to Madeline's mother. That bit of information, carelessly given, added to its mystique. Her mother had treated it as her most prized possession. Every day she made Eugenie polish the surface with cedar oil she bought from Devaux's store.

This was the main bedroom in the house. It had been her mother's. Eugenie told Madeline her mother had given birth to her in that room. She claimed to remember the event since she had been the midwife, and had delivered Madeline on her own, even though her father had asked a doctor to be present. As far as she was concerned, he need not have been there because he had done nothing to earn his fee.

"He didn have to stay," she said. "He didn do noffing, just stan up lookin toutoulbé – like he confuse. When he see you wid dat nice black mark roun you eye he shout 'Oh Gawd!' You mama get a kwiz onetime. He tell your papa is somefing I do. Me! Is me dat tek care of you mama. Is me dat mek she get better. I don know why he shout like dat. He mek you mama sick. An you deh, so pretty wif your beautiful mark."

Madeline had moved into the room when her mother had died soon after she had been taken to the asylum. One day she discovered a mirror that was almost identical to the one on the bureau. It was framed in mahogany and there were carvings of leaves in the wood but no grapes. She was amazed at the similarity and had bought it. Despite Eugenie's protestations about bad luck, she hung it on the wall opposite the bureau. This made the room seem larger.

She looked at Evon in the mirror. She could see the front and back of him replicated in a series of fractured images, as though he were transfixed in several dimensions. They were looking directly at each other but in different mirrors. She broke the silence with a hollow laugh.

"It's the money, isn't it?" She tilted her head, willing him to focus on her. He blinked and looked away. "You've withdrawn since I told you I couldn't give you more money. Is that it? Evon, this gambling is destroying you. I'm not helping by giving you money whenever you ask for it. I'd hoped you'd realize that. Stay. Let's work this through."

"Don't patronize me, Madeline. It's not the money. I can do without it. I said I'd pay you back. I will."

"What about everything you said? If it isn't the money what is it? It's my eye, isn't it?" She was pleading. She hated it, but wanted to get under the armour he had crafted to exclude her. It wasn't the thought that he seemed to have become indifferent that irritated her; it was the possibility that he had been interested in her money and not her. He was silent for a moment. Then he said, "Madeline, face reality. Look at us. Look in the mirror. This won't work."

She jumped out of bed, went to the bureau, peering into the mirror at the black patch that covered her left eye, like a harlequin's mask. It started beneath her eyebrow, fully covering her eyelid, tapering to the corner of her eye at the bridge of her nose, circling the hollow beneath her eye, narrowing into a thin line at her temple. She had grown used to people staring at her, wanting to discover whether she had a patch over her eye, then looking away quickly when they realized it was her skin.

"You used to say you liked my eye. You called me your 'B-B'. If it isn't my eye, what is it, then?" He didn't answer but turned away, opened the closet and started removing his clothes from it. She sat on the edge of the bed, staring into the mirror. She recalled that he hadn't looked away when he first saw her. He had stepped purposefully out of the manager's booth in the supermarket on the corner. He had walked up to her with an audacity that threw her off balance and said "You're beautiful." He reached up and touched her eye. She felt it had caught fire beneath his touch. She had left abruptly and gone home, gravitating to the mirror when she got there to look at her eye.

She had always thought this nevus her attraction. Her mother and Eugenie had stressed that, despite taunts she occasionally got from youths on the corner. "Ga led-la" – "Look the ugly one" someone might call and the others would whistle or shout "Black eye!" Eugenie told her they were jealous. She believed this. She would toss her head, stride down the sidewalk, the wind blowing her skirt against her legs. Madeline seemed indifferent to what people thought about her looks. She was tall, and wore her hair in an Afro that accentuated the lines of her face and the nevus on her eye.

Evon's bold encounter was the start of something that became more intense with each visit to the supermarket. He made a point of bagging her groceries and when he had finished he would put his fingertip against her eye and say "My B-B."

"I'm not your baby. Stop it."

"You're my Beautiful Black eye," he would retort, laughing. He did this with such charm she knew pretence at being offended would have made her seem churlish. She looked forward to her visits to the supermarket. On one of those visits, he offered to carry her groceries and she had let him. After that day, he would stop by after work sometimes and they would sit on the veranda talking, sipping rum punch Eugenie had made. Sometimes he would stay to supper. With each visit his hour of leaving was later until he didn't leave. Once in a while he would go off to play cards, he said, and Madeline would lend him money when he ran out.

She recalled this as she stared into the mirror, seeing his reflection repeated infinitely refracted with each successive image replicated in the mirrors. She worried about why he decided to leave; worried that it could be because of the one reason she had hesitated to mention. She couldn't bear the thought of it.

"Is it because of what I told you last night? I shouldn't have, but I thought you'd want to know." She looked up at him and touched his arm. He pulled away and turned back to the closet.

"It's bad enough that you did what you did but to blame it on me by saying I didn't want children . . ." He shook his head.

"You said so. You said so more than once, Evon. I didn't want to lose you."

"It was part of both of us, Madeline."

"Don't go." He pulled away and moved towards the door. She got up and moved closer to him. She held his arm and looked directly into his eyes. She was as tall as he was, something he used to say he liked because they fit well together.

"I can't stay knowing this and what you and Eugenie did."

"Don't blame her, Evon. I was feeling ill. She looked at me and said something about a baby. I didn't know, and didn't understand how she could tell . . . I blurted out that you didn't want children. She's taken care of me my whole life, Evon. The tea she gave me helped to calm me. I didn't know it would have that effect. She knew how anxious I was . . . I shouldn't have told you anything . . . I don't even know if it was the tea . . ."

"You'd be better off if you didn't listen to that old witch." He reached for the doorknob. The buzzing in her ears which started whenever she was agitated grew louder. Her heart thumped. She was furious with herself for having allowed him to break through defences she had built. Three years with him had been blissful. She had tolerated the censure of friends who said she was degrading herself by becoming the mistress of a drifter from "No-one-knew-where". She liked his boldness, his caressing her eye and calling her his B-B. She had surrendered to him with an intensity of feeling. She had lost a part of him and now she was losing him too.

Who in this small town, she wondered, would look at her, a woman with a black eye – a nevus that was permanent? A woman who had lived with an outsider. A woman who had been discarded. She was agitated, distracted. She leaned against the bureau, felt the handle of her hand- mirror and grasped it, wishing its solidity would restore her equilibrium. At the door he turned to her and said, "Get a life, Madeline." She hurled the hand-mirror across the room. It missed him and shattered against the door. He was shaken. He stared at her and said, "You're unhinged!" Through the buzzing in her ears the slamming of the door was muffled.

She went to the door. She thought she heard Eugenie calling her. She was on the other side, waiting for a word before she came in. She heard her mother saying that shattering a mirror would bring bad luck and sadness.

"As if I care," she muttered as she stooped to pick up some of the splinters. She opened the door; Eugenie was standing there. Madeline hardly heard what she said.

"Didn I tell you he no good? Doudou, don mek yourself sick over dat séléwa! He no good, you hear? He like George, dat rascal dat turn your mother head. Sit down, doudou." She led Madeline into the front room.

❦

Madeline sat in the armchair facing the large mirror, another of her mother's prized possessions. It hung where she had placed it, facing the door so she could see her reflection whenever she entered the room. The tain was worn around the edges and in the middle. This made it seem as though she were looking into a pool – a calm sea – at the centre.

"Sit down, shéwi," Eugenie cooed. She pried Madeline's hand open and removed the splinters which had cut her. "Bon Dyé, look what you do. You goin kill yourself for dat engwa? He ungrateful!" She mopped the blood from Madeline's palm.

You lied telling me I was pretty. Why did you preen in front of that mirror, caressing your belly, giving me this birth mark? Why didn't you make Papa stay? Why did you leave me with this longing to be like you, this longing to be loved? Why was I born with this? I'm sorry I made the mistake with the broom. Papa loved you. He would have stayed if it wasn't for George. He loved me too. Evon's B-B talk was a joke. Now he's gone, like you, like Papa . . .

A peal of thunder rolled through the fog in her head. The gramophone scraped to a halt. The music stopped. The rain was pelting down outside. Another flash of lightning; the mirror cracked. She blinked. In its fractured surface she saw the door opening, and her mother sweeping through it, her reflection walking towards Madeline through the tunnel. She was smiling, holding out her arms. She stood up, reaching out to her mother's reflection. Another blinding flash of lightning and her mother's image seemed to fade as George and Evon walked in. They were laughing.

"Liars!" she shouted. She walked towards the mirror as another flash of lightning lit up the empty room. She blinked as the two seemed to fade into the pool.

Madeline grasped the mirror and dashed it against the wall, laughing as their faces disintegrated in shards at her feet. She opened the door and strode into the storm towards the track leading to their favourite cove.

The Flowering of Rosa

One night she dreamt that the top of her head had blossomed into a flower and someone had watered it. She woke to find pools gathered at the corners of her eyes; they rolled down her cheeks. Hamish opened his eyes at that moment and said,

"Why, Rosa, you're crying. What's wrong?"

She wiped away the tiny rivulets. "It's the watering, don't you see? Nothing's wrong, everything's right today."

"I see." Hamish wasn't sure that he could see, but he moved closer to her, wanting to enter her dream, that part of her waking that bemused him as she let him slip into her imaginings and live in her dreams of the night before.

On the previous morning he had watched *as she stepped out on the balcony of her grandmother's house – carrying her little girl in her arms – He had watched as – out of nowhere – a brown bull charged at her from behind – Its right horn lodged between her left arm and body, and he could sense her fear for the child whose face lay against her arm – The bull tossed its head and she was thrown free – She lifted the child who smiled at her – its smooth, plump cheeks dimpling.*

At the time he had made a mental note to buy some stocks or a lottery ticket later in the day. A bull in her dream must mean luck, he had thought. He wasn't perturbed that he hadn't been in that dream.

"I forgot to buy a ticket," he said.

"What ticket?"

"Lottery. Thought we might be in for some luck."

"We've been lucky only you can't see it." She shifted to her left, away from him slightly, and the scent of roses filled the room. He longed to draw nearer, to press his face against her breasts, absorb her fragrances; mists of rose, essence of gardenias, whiffs of crushed forget-me-nots. There, he could imagine himself in a garden blinded by the colour of her eyes, drunk with the fragrance of her.

"You never told me the rest of your dream," he said. "You stopped at the part with the bull."

After the bull disappeared I went to my mother's house; it's not far from Grandma's just up the road a bit – It seems she was planning an entertainment – some people were there already – and she was putting last-minute touches –

'You're joining us?' she asked.

'I've got to see Father John; he's leaving tomorrow.'

'Can't stay still for one minute, can you?' she said – shaking her head. 'Always going here – hurrying there – We hardly get to see you anymore.'

'I'll be back as soon as I can – You know Father John promised to let me have that painting – the one I liked – He'll be puzzled if I don't show up – I'll walk quickly and won't be long' – I found myself walking up the Calvary Road – then I thought that it would take me a long time to get to the rectory in Barbados from Calvary in Saint Lucia and I was stupid to walk when the old car was parked in front of the house – I went back for the car – but, as I set out again, a riot had erupted in the street – Someone had closed the gates at the end of our street and I could only inch towards them – They were straining against the crush of the mob – This time Katie was with me – She had begged me to let her go along. You know how persistent she can be sometimes. I had said yes; but now she was crouched low in her seat trembling – her eyes wide with fear – I grabbed her hand – opened the door and we ran off – I thought that I would get the car later if it was still there – Somehow we got to the rectory. I can't remember how we got there; but I was knocking on the door and someone told me that Father John had gone to bed – I could see his bare legs sticking out over the edge of the bed – He woke up and came towards me.

'I'm glad you came – I wanted to tell you about the painting – Do you like it?'

'Yes – It's interesting how it suggests the crucifixion without the cross – You know – with his arms extended and his feet crossed.'

'He's risen and his grace is pouring out over the landscape in golden bands of light – See – he's also the puppeteer – Look how the figures of Mary and John are suspended from his arms by the bands of light and dancing to his tune.'

'Yes – I see – and his grace also rises from the earth to meet them – It's wonderful.'

'Perhaps it will help you to remember that his grace hasn't left you – it isn't far from you – You must look into the sunrises and through the sunsets.'

Then in the dream I remembered another reason I had gone to see Father John so I said – 'But my dreams – they haunt me – I remember two of them clearly' – He came to the door and knocked – I was pleased to see him but I closed the door and I don't ever remember opening it –

"For some strange reason I always seem to be paralysed in these dreams – I had the first one when I was eight – just around the time of my first communion – I used to be a flower girl in the May and October processions – I was small so they let me walk beside the float and hold one of the blue ribbons that were attached to it – They let the smaller girls do that – There were no boys around the float – they walked in the procession with everybody else – Three of the bigger girls walked directly behind the float throwing rose petals towards the crowds from small wicker baskets that they carried – One – two – three steps forward – turn right throw petals – step – turn right throw at the Virgin Mary on the float – one – two – three steps forward and start over.

"I wanted to do that very much – They always let the Montpelier girls do that – They were bigger than the rest of us and they were identical twins – They were also fair with straight hair that fell below their shoulders – Every year I used to wish that they would have disappeared – been sent to boarding school so the ribbon holders would have a chance to throw rose petals – I could imagine myself doing it – One – two – three steps forward – turn right – throw to the crowd – one – two – three steps –

turn right again and throw to the virgin on the float – She would look down at me from the height of the float resting on the shoulders of four young women – They were all dressed in white – with white veils over their heads – I imagined they were all virgins – The statue would shake ever so slightly from the unevenness of their heights even though their shoulders were padded with layers of cloth to make up the difference and to keep them from getting bruised.

"They walked slowly – carefully – and we walked beside the float slowly but not as carefully while the crowds sang in looping notes – those in the second half of the procession singing two bars behind those in the first half who were three or four blocks ahead – 'Oh sinless heart all hail / God's dear delight all hail'."

In the dream, the sunlight suddenly seemed more intense and I began to feel uncomfortable – All the while the scent of roses filled the hot afternoon air and I was dizzy with it and acutely aware of the hot asphalt burning through the soles of the new shoes my mother had bought for the occasion – Toes blistering in the too-tight shoes – skin irritated from the can-can half-petticoat that billowed beneath the organdie skirt – itching – sticking into my waist at every step – I wanted to reach up and pluck the wreath of white roses from my head – step into the crowd at the side of the road and disappear – One – two – three – step – turn and a shower of petals falling from the float on me – I looked up to see the statue's eyes gazing at me and the brows seemed to gather in a frown –

"That same night I had the first dream – that I shut the door when he came to visit."

'These are just dreams,' Father John said – 'Your anxieties surfacing in your moments of deepest rest – Remember, look into the sunrises and through the sunsets' –

"I can't remember what happened after I left Father John's, but I remember wondering what he meant about looking into the sunrises and through the sunsets."

Suddenly I was back home and mingling with my mother's friends and I thought that I hadn't even told him about the second dream, about when I shut the door a second time. I wanted to go back and tell him, but I didn't.

"I remember the dream well enough though."

I was in a room – it must have been night time – it was dark outside – The light inside the room shed a warm golden glow – I was restless – I remember walking up and down in the room – pacing the floor – I could hear the wind blowing strongly outside – The curtains hanging over the single window were billowing inwards – the tattered hems making a buzzing sound like the tail of a kite in the wind – I can't remember why I was restless – Then I heard a knock on the door and I walked towards it and opened the top half – It was one of those doors which were in two parts so you could open the top like a window. The bottom half was latched. There was a fine wire mesh screen across the top half – the sort of screen they use to keep bugs out – or like the screen over the window of a confessional box – As I moved to the door I remember thinking how much like a confessional the top half looked – I opened it and he was standing there – I knew he was the one because of the beard and the eyes – They were exactly like the image my mother had hanging on one of the walls in her bedroom – I was surprised to see his face, but at the same time I had a feeling of satisfaction as though I had been expecting the visit and all the restlessness vanished – His face was expressionless and he said nothing – He just stood there quietly – waiting for me to let him in – I mumbled something – perhaps about opening the door – but I had to close the top half first – I did that – then something in the room distracted me and I went to look – I didn't open the door right away – By the time I remembered – I ran to open it and he had gone –

"When I woke the next morning, I was disturbed by the dream. It worried me for days. I thought over and over about what might have led me to dream that, but I couldn't come up with anything. I mean, I couldn't think of anything that I had done. I just had a general restlessness, a feeling that I was missing out on something, but I couldn't say what.

"That was before I met you, Hamy. I was young then, somewhere in my early twenties and I was enjoying life. I had a great set of friends. We used to meet every Friday afternoon in a bar, Gee's bar which overlooked a narrow back street of the town. We retreated there after work to get away from the heat of the Friday afternoon busyness. We would sit in the air-conditioned coolness and Richard, my poet friend who exaggeratedly played the role of poet would order the first round of beer. He'd take out a packet of cigarettes, offer them round, then light each one. We did all this in a sort of reverent silence waiting while he took the first drag. He'd inhale deeply and say 'nicotine, nicotine' and we'd smile and nod. I remember the tingling in my body after that first inhalation, the rush to my head that made me dizzy and the tart taste of that first sip of ice-cold beer. Gee always served us the first round himself. It was a kind of ritual – the cigarettes, the first sip of beer. After that beginning, we'd all start talking at once.

"In those days I used to look forward to Friday afternoons. I fancied that Richard and I were in love, in an intellectual sort of way; it all took place in the mind. I don't remember if we ever touched, I don't think we did, but I knew everything there was to know about him. For instance, I knew why he dedicated a particular poem to a particular girl and why he was driven to pursue a particular other. I knew that he secretly dreamt of being a priest, more because of the mystery of the office than from a desire to serve. Richard couldn't have been celibate in those days for a day if he tried. He used to say two words together often, 'priest' and 'poet'. I think he even wrote the phrase as a line in one of his poems. He'd say it with reverence, a far-away look in his eyes, as though he were seeing himself robed in an alb and preaching poems from a pulpit. He used to admire Peter, our mutual friend who had become a priest and who had known from the day that he was born that this was what he wanted to be.

"In those days I fancied myself a poet too; I guess we all did. Our Friday afternoon meetings affirmed that we were a cult, a cult of would-be poets. I used to write poems about sunrises, sunsets, moonlight, love and roses, poems that were fashioned after the Romantics because their poetry was all we used to read at school in those days. I had a notebook full of poems. I never shared them with the others; Peter would read from 'Chalice of Love', a long poem which he wrote about his vocation, a poem about pure, unspoiled love for the priesthood, for God, I suppose. When I went away the first time, a real poet asked me to let him see my poems and I did, hesitantly. I remember waiting uncomfortably for his verdict because I had started to read T.S. Eliot, Yeats, Auden and Walcott, and somehow sunsets and roses, at least, the way I used to write about them, seemed far away from the stuff of modern poetry.

"He gave me back the book with notes scribbled over it, and at the end he had written one line, 'Daddy, daddy you bastard, I'm through.' It was only later when I started reading Plath that I discovered where that line came from, and I understood its significance. It might have been all in my mind, but afterwards I used to think that he treated me with a kind of contempt. There was another girl who wrote poetry. She was in his class, and I knew that he thought of her as a real poet. At readings he would sit, adoringly, at her feet and light her cigarettes while she sat on a stool puffing dutifully and reading in accented tones. After that I limited my encounters with poetry to reading it. I read a lot of Richard's poetry. He was publishing them in magazines and he used to ask me to read them first. I shared poetry with Richard and secrets with Peter.

"I had stopped smoking because of the coughing and I had become more studied, less spontaneous. I was more careful about the secrets I told Peter, and I treated these confidences as sacred confessions until I discovered that he had betrayed me when he told a particular secret, a confession, to Richard, who blurted it out to my face one day when we stood talking with a friend in front of the cathedral. That betrayal scarred me. I had never expected it of Peter who seemed to be so devoted to his vocation. I couldn't imagine him ever breaking a trust. I stopped telling him secrets altogether, and I didn't speak to him for a very long time. I think that was the time the dream recurred. I never did get to tell Father John about it, but I hadn't really told him about the first one either, I had only told it to him in a dream. It's funny, but sometimes when I wake up I can't tell whether I dreamt these things or whether they really happened. Sometimes I can hardly tell the difference between my dreams and reality."

Hamish stirred slightly. He could hear her voice from far away. He realized that he must have dozed off and now he woke again to the soft drone of her voice. He wasn't quite sure what she had been saying. He liked to listen to her. Her voice calmed a deep restlessness in him, a restlessness which had become more intense in recent days. He didn't know the cause of it. He opened his mouth to speak, to tell Rosa about it, but he thought better of it. Lately she had seemed distant, didn't register his presence with the enthusiasm of old. She had seemed to change right after his harmless flirtation with Meiling, the Chinese girl who worked in his office. He knew it was harmless, but Rosa didn't. At first, she would question him when he got home late and then she had withdrawn. It was a gradual thing; he hadn't realized it was happening until now it suddenly occurred to him that these moments when she told him of her dreams and the events that they prompted her to recall were their only moments of intimacy. He could only encounter the real her in her dreams, in the stories that she told him when she woke up. Even then, he felt like a spectator looking on at her from a distance in a world that was peopled with characters he didn't know. He felt almost like a stranger because she never seemed to have dreams in which he featured, or if she did she never told him about them.

Hamish felt a nagging uneasiness that he'd felt frequently in recent times that he was losing Rosa. He couldn't pin down any specific thing she had said or any different behaviour. It just seemed to him that she was less accessible to him than before, although physically she was there as she had always been, as she was now, beside him. Yet she was remote, withdrawn into a world that was a secret part of herself where he seemed unable to follow or reach her. She stirred slightly and the scent of roses mushroomed over the bed.

"Is that a new perfume, Rosa?"

"Perfume? What perfume?"

"The one you're wearing. It's new, isn't it?"

"It's the usual, but I didn't put on any last night."

"It seems stronger, like flowers in a garden. Thought it was new."

He pressed his face against her arm. The smell of roses was overpowering; he felt dizzy with it. He could feel the tiny hairs on her arm like small thorns sticking into his cheek. He drew back hastily and lay looking up at the ceiling. He thought he should get up, get ready for work, but it was still dark outside and much too early to begin the day.

"Are you awake?" He woke just in time to hear the question and realized that he must have drifted off.

"We were speaking of gardens, weren't we?"

"No. Perfume. You said my perfume smelled like a garden."

"Yes. Lately, the whole room smells like a garden. Sometimes the scent is so strong I feel dizzy, almost sick with it. Don't you smell it too?"

"No, I don't. But I often dream that I'm in a garden. Sometimes, I'm a flower, most often, a rose. Earlier I dreamt that I was a rose in a garden and the gardener had left the sprinklers on. I was dripping and I reached up to touch my forehead and it was dripping too. There was so much water, I felt as though I was drowning, like the time I was a little girl and I had gone to the beach with my parents. We used to go early in the morning, around five o'clock. The beach was deserted then, the sand smooth and cleanly swept by the night's waves. We used to dig deep holes. Sometimes, we would bury each other in them, leaving only our heads sticking out above the sand. That morning I went into the water and there was a sudden drop. I went under, then came up gasping for air and I couldn't feel the sand. I went under again, swallowing a mouthful of water. When I surfaced, I could see the hibiscus hedge in the lane at the back of our house. I used to walk there every day on my way to and from school. Sometimes, I would pick the flowers and we would crush them with the leaves to make soapy water to wash our hair. We would rub the thick oily liquid in, leaves and all, until it lathered, and then we would rinse it out with rainwater. Sometimes we crushed rose petals in the water too. Our hair would smell like flowers and I would feel special, like a flower.

"As I came up gasping for air, I could see the hedge, bright red with flowers. You know, it's true what they say. When you're drowning you see things and reach for them. I saw that hibiscus hedge clearly, but of course, it wasn't really there. I lunged forward, grabbing at a branch, but it seemed to be just out of reach and I went under again. I came up gasping, choking, thinking that if I could grab the branch I'd be safe. I lunged for the hedge again – the flowers were redder than I'd ever seen them and all full blown. As I was going under, a hand pulled me up by the arm. It was my sister and she was calling to my parents. They came and got me out. I've always wondered why I imagined that particular hedge. It was so real I felt I could touch it. But the more I reached for the flowers, the closer I was to drowning.

"After that I learned to swim and in my dreams I could breathe under the water, in the curl of a wave or underneath, close to the seabed. Since then I've never been afraid of the water or of drowning. I've often dreamt of the sea. Did I tell you my sea dreams, Hamy?" Hamish reached out to draw her near. She felt the weight of his arm and moved away slightly. He leaned forward to press his face to her breast and again he felt the tiny hairs on her arms, and her skin was moist. He was light-headed with the smell of roses.

"You started to tell me about your garden dreams."

"Oh those." She chuckled softly. "Those were not such good dreams because they always had snakes in them. You know how mortally afraid I am of snakes. I remember three dreams like that but now that I think about them, only the last one had a garden in it. How confusing this is."

"Tell me anyway," Hamish said sleepily, running his finger along her arm and thinking how cool her skin was. He shivered.

"Hamy?"

"Hmm?"

"Know what I've been dreaming about lately? I've been thinking how nice it would be to go away to someplace quiet, someplace with only a few people – perhaps a small island where I could be alone, swim, read; not have to do anything I didn't want to do."

"Where would I be, and Katie?"

"Oh, you could come if you wanted to, you know that." He pressed his cheek against her arm. "It would be like before, before we got too busy to feel or to remember the good times. An island with a good beach like the one I dreamt about the other day. Don't you remember? I told you about it."

I had taken Katie to the beach and she got away – I couldn't find her – I thought she had gone in the water and I dived in – There were tall waves but I wasn't afraid – I went right through one of them and as it broke over me I found myself flying and looking down on the beach – Katie was there playing with some friends and I called out to her but she couldn't hear me – I don't think I made any sound –

"Strange, I never used to dream that I could fly. You were always the one who had those dreams. Remember how I laughed when you first told me you dreamt you had been flying? You said you were in some sort of danger and you spread your arms and flew."

"I don't have those dreams anymore," Hamish said. "Don't know when I last had a flying dream. I used to enjoy them, though, it was great, soaring above everything, gliding along a current of air. I had such a feeling of freedom."

"That's exactly how I felt in the dream; free, liberated. I could have kept going forever."

"You stole my dream, Rosa," he said.

"What?"

"You stole my . . . nothing." He knew it wouldn't do any good to repeat what he'd said. It would only start an argument for which he didn't have the energy. But he couldn't suppress a feeling of resentment towards Rosa, a feeling that she had trespassed onto his territory and had robbed him of something valuable. Hers were dreams of gardens, the sea, waves, snakes and bearded visitors. His used to be dreams of flying. He couldn't understand the significance of her dreams, but he knew that they had assumed some importance in their lives, had somehow begun to define their relationship, and he had an uncanny feeling that their entire future was bound up in these dreams. Why else, he thought, would he have that strange compulsion to lie beside her morning after morning listening to her recount her dreams of the night before and their connection to her life and to dreams she'd had before, some even when she was a child? Sometimes he found it difficult to make the connection between what was real and what dream as she wove threads from dreams and memories creating a tapestry that each day revealed more and more of her and yet seemed to distance her from him.

There were times when he thought he understood her well, that she was allowing him to discover her in ways that he had not thought possible. And yet, at those times, when he reached for her, she seemed most distant from him and he felt excluded from her life. Now he was resentful, but remonstrated with himself for being stupid. It was ridiculous to think that she could "steal" his dreams of flying. She had her dreams and he, his; at least the ones he could remember most vividly, his flying dreams. But he hadn't had one of these for ages. It seemed that they had stopped right after Rosa had first told him about her first flying dream, the one when she had dived through a wave, spread her arms and flown clear out of the water. She had woken up right afterwards to tell him about it and he had felt cheated, as though Rosa had robbed him of something precious. Since then he had never had one of those dreams. Instead, he became caught up in the tapestry that Rosa wove each day, fearing that if he missed an episode he would miss an important happening in their lives.

"I didn't steal anything, Hamish. Don't you remember? You told me how simple it was to fly, that I just needed to think it, spread my arms and I would fly. That's all I did." She could feel beads of water gathering on her forehead and at the corners of her eyes. Lately she found it difficult to understand Hamish. He seemed absorbed in another world, a world of ledgers and numbers and it seemed that his only dreams were about winning the lottery. She thought herself a fool for telling him her dreams because she was sure he slept all the while she was talking. Even now, he couldn't stay awake to hear her answer. He had fallen off to sleep again and snored lightly beside her. She told herself that she didn't much care if he didn't hear anything. She had started to tell him about the recurring dream she had been having of their being lost in a house that was submerged.

When she first had the dream, they had been swimming in a rooftop pool which was in the middle of a garden –

There were luxuriant hedges around the pool and she remembered thinking that strange – There were rose bushes entwined with the hibiscus and the flowers were wonderfully bright – Then she dived and found herself in a house with many doors – Hamish was beside her and they were trying to find their way out – He would open a door and disappear into a room and she would open another and swim through only to come face to face with Hamish – They would swim together for a while and then open other doors only to have the same thing happen – She felt trapped in the dream – each door seemed to lead backwards to where she had been before and there she would encounter Hamish who was trapped too.

A cool breeze drifted in through the window. It smelt of a garden after rain and she could feel a moistness in the air. It settled on her face and she could feel the moisture gathering again at the corners of her eyes. Hamish's arm lay heavily across her. She shifted uneasily and turned on her side. Hamish stirred, moved closer to her; touched her cheek.

"What's the matter, Rosa? You're crying again."

"Did I tell you about the strange dream I had the other night? The one in which we were trapped in the submerged house?"

"Yes, you told me you dreamt it twice." He tried to put his arm around Rosa, but she had moved away from him to the other side of the bed and now she lay with her back to him like a wall. He rolled over on his stomach and pressed his face into her pillow. That was slightly damp too, and smelt of flowers. He clutched the pillow tightly, feeling that if he let go, he would be lost.

Rosa dreamt she was in the house again and she opened a door and could see a small patch of light at the top of a stairway – She swam back into the room and beckoned to Hamish who was about to open another door – She motioned to him to follow then began to swim up the stairway – She looked back for Hamish but he wasn't following – He had gone back to the other door and was about to swim through – Rosa went to him and tugged his shirt – He turned to follow her and she swam up the stairway again – She turned round to look for Hamish again but he wasn't following – He was treading water in the middle of the room and looking at her doubtfully – his head slightly tilted to one side – She stopped for a moment then turned and continued swimming up the stairwell as fast as she could go – keeping her eyes on the square of light above – The flowers from the hedges had blown onto the surface of the pool and the bright flowers were floating in eddies made by the wind – She broke the surface, flowers covering her hair – She could feel the gooey sap from the hibiscus coating her skin and seeping into her pores – Above her she could see the blue expanse of sky and the sun hovering low over the hills – She stared at it, remembering vaguely something someone had said to her about sunrises and sunsets in a dream that she had had – She tried to wipe away the film of sap from her eyes but it clung to her eyelashes and she could see the sun magnified – a deep orange ball hanging above the hills – Its rays seemed to penetrate her skin and she felt herself absorbing it – every cell tingling with the warmth of it until she felt a deep relaxation as though her body had been freed from its casing of skin so that her entire body was now pliant like a young shoot – She felt the wind blowing through the leaves of her hair and lifting her out of the water – with the roses and hibiscus clinging to her – and bearing her on a warm current into the heart of the sun – As she surrendered herself completely to the gentle force that bore her to what she thought was her destiny – she made a mental note that she should remember to tell Hamish about this dream when she woke and to reassure him that he could have his flying dreams again because she had discovered something better.

Hamish had a falling sensation and woke suddenly. A cool breeze blew in through the open window. He shivered. He reached across for Rosa, but his arm fell across the empty space where she had been lying. The scent of flowers was overpowering. Hamish turned on his back and looked out the window. The sky was a perfect blue; there wasn't a cloud that he could see. Above the hills the sun was rising. In the distance, far out against the sun, he thought that he could see something moving but he couldn't tell exactly what it was, it was too far away. But he had the strongest feeling that if he ran to the window and stretched out his arms, he would be able to fly just as he used to do in his dreams. He had such a feeling of elation that he wanted to share it with Rosa to reassure her that he knew he could still fly in his dreams. He was intoxicated with the smell of roses that filled the room. He turned over and pressed his face into the indentation that Rosa's head had made in her pillow. He turned, looked out towards the sun again and wished that he was that speck against the sun; it was much closer now and he thought that it looked like a flower, a rose, carried high on a current of air. Again, he felt a strong urge to fly, and he thought that if he did he would be borne on the wind and he would fly as easily as he used to in his dreams. He got out of bed, taking deep breaths, feeling light-headed, light all over. He walked purposefully towards the window, then stopped suddenly as the alarm went off. For a moment he seemed confused, unsure about whether he should continue to the window. Then he remembered that it was his turn to take Katie to school. He stood there for a long moment looking longingly towards the sun which was now high above the hill and so bright he could not look at it or see the object which he knew was there drifting towards him on the wind. As he turned reluctantly to dress for work he reminded himself that he should tell Rosa about this. He made a mental note that he should buy a ticket because it seemed to him a perfect day for winning the lottery.

Mav's Meditations

My name is Florette Mavis Montoute but everyone calls me Mav. I prefer Florette; it has a flowery sound but I suppose Mav is easier to remember. I got to like it more after Arnold and I met and he started calling me Marvellous Mav. He used to stress the *Marv* part so it sounded like Mahvlus Mahv. Sometimes he called me Mav my all – his translation of my family name, Montoute. That's cute and I like it. Our first seven years together were marvellous. First the courting, then the wedding, then living together. It was as if we were trying to outdo each other in finding small ways to please. I discovered early that Arnold can be moody sometimes, but after a while, I learned not to pay too much attention to that and to stay out of his way when he is in one of his moods. He refers to the moods as his state of melancholic gloom; as if melancholy is not gloom. I know a mood is coming on when he starts to call me Mavis. It's Mavis this and Mavis that. Two months ago, one of his moods came on and it's so bad this time that he sits at his laptop for hours on end. When he turns that off, he's glued to his mobile phone. That's all he seems to want to do when he's at home. He holds on to his phone as if his life depends upon it. We've been living as though we are two islands in a wide sea, distant from each other but occasionally feeling a ripple from the current flowing between our shores. This is the first time his gloom has lasted this long.

I told my friend Rita about this latest one and that set her off on a long story about the benefit of meditating consistently. I'm sure she said that to make me feel guilty because I've been meditating on and off. I haven't been enthusiastic about it because I can't ever seem to feel the bliss and peace Rita says she gets whenever she meditates. Before I met Arnold, Rita and I had gone to a presentation on Transcendental Meditation, more out of curiosity than anything else. We decided to get initiated into TM and a youngish Chinese man, Charles, had prepared us for the ceremony. He was meticulous about the preparations, giving us small bouquets of hibiscus to take in to the teacher who saw us individually to teach us the method and give us our mantras. Afterwards, Charles would call me to find out how my meditations were going and he would offer suggestions about what I should do to transcend. It wasn't long before we started dating.

We would go swimming in the late afternoon and do yoga asanas on the grass in the coconut grove next to the beach. The swimming and asanas made me fit and Charles would tell me how good I looked. I guess it's this look that attracted Arnold. While our routine gave me good looks and I felt healthy, it did not affect my mind much. Whenever we settled down to meditate my mind would take flight and thoughts would come in to nest, hop around and chase each other in quick succession. After every session when we meditated together, we seemed to have a conversation along the same lines, beginning with Charles asking me about transcending.

"Did you transcend?"

"No, but my mind is lighter now. You'll have to tell me what transcendence is like and how it feels so I can tell you truthfully."

"I guess the experience is different for each person, but you know it when you have it. A lassitude gradually creeps over you and you lose sense of time, of your physical self. Then there's a feeling of elation that lifts your mind, heart and spirit to another realm."

"Well, I have lots of thoughts. They come one after another and I'm involved with them. I even have conversations with the people in them."

"That's not it. You're distracted. Remember, when thoughts come, set them aside firmly and repeat your mantra. Focus on it."

So it went on, and I was happy with Charles for a few months until his group had to go away. I missed our routines and after a while I stopped meditating. Rita said if I hadn't stopped, I would manage things much better when Arnold gets depressed. She has stuck with her practice and she assures me that her meditations lead to bliss. She often asks me to join her group, but I'm in no frame of mind to join a group of meditation enthusiasts who discuss the ecstasy they experience after a session. But I must admit I need something to quell my discomfort with Arnold's growing detachment. I told Rita I would join later, but would try to get back into it on my own first. I'm serious about this because the last thing I want to do is fixate on the rift that seems to be growing between Arnold and me.

It is now several weeks that I have been trying. I remember the instructions the TM teacher and Charles had given me, and I've been doing my best to observe them in twenty-minute sessions in the morning and evening. I repeat the mantra but as soon as I sit down and close my eyes, the thoughts come flying in and I'm awash in a sea of distractions.

One afternoon, Rita called to say that a teacher would be visiting and I agreed to go along in case she showed a technique that would give me a breakthrough. I went and there was Nasrine in flowing, flower-patterned robes, sitting cross-legged in a full lotus position and smiling benignly as though she had achieved the height of spiritual enlightenment. The group members, the devotees, had brought blossoms which they placed at Nasrine's feet before they bowed, palms pressed together and whispered a reverent greeting. Nasrine spoke about her visit to India and her stay at an ashram where she had learned to "conquer the desires of the flesh" and had achieved mystical bliss. She talked about her guru and as she gestured and moved her hands and head, she seemed to take on a different persona; or so it seemed to me. I whispered this to Rita who said I was being silly. She hissed at me to be quiet and sat with her eyes closed. At the end, Nasrine invited questions and I asked her how she controlled thoughts during meditation. Perhaps it was the wrong way to ask the question because she interpreted it to mean that I assumed she was plagued with thoughts when she meditated.

"Child," she said in a condescending tone, "thoughts do not bother me at all." She waved her hand as though with a flick of her wrist she was able to bat away intrusive thoughts. "I have achieved such discipline that my mind goes into a totally different space as soon as I close my eyes." She was generous enough to share some tips on what had helped her achieve discipline. "Grounding is the best thing," she said, pointing the fingers of both hands to the ground. "You have to be grounded before you begin to repeat the mantra or the thoughts will persist. There are different ways to be grounded but one of my favourites is to imagine myself as being rooted to the earth, like a tree. Imagine roots shooting from your feet, piercing the earth and clinging to it. When you do that, you can focus better on repeating your mantra and managing your thoughts. That will begin your path to enlightenment and the heightening of your consciousness."

Since that meeting, I've been using this grounding technique. I don't think it can do any harm. After all, I've been trying to meditate for a long time and I haven't had even the slightest glimpse into this space where a person is supposed to be overcome with bliss. Rita has been encouraging. "The dynamic may be a catalyst for the focus and attention you need," she says. I'm still hesitant about her group because I don't want to participate in the after-session discussions where I will have to describe my experience. What if it's the same old thing? I can still remember the discussion we had in the session after our initiation. One of the men who was initiated on the same morning reported afterwards that he had a "mind-blowing" experience in which with each repetition of the mantra he felt himself rise until he was poised above his body and looking down at himself as he meditated. At the time, I told Rita that I didn't believe him and he was making it up to impress the teacher. But I may have been wrong. Perhaps astral travelling was the form of transcendence he was experiencing. Who am I to decide what is possible for anyone? Since those days I've been meditating in solitude and now

I keep up a discipline of daily meditations. That's an improvement, so I tell myself that I'm getting better at it and one of these days I'll reach the height of bliss and spiritual enlightenment that Rita speaks about.

Over the last four weeks in particular, I've kept my resolution because it seems that Arnold is too deep in gloom to pay me any mind. One morning I woke up early and got out of bed quietly because Arnold had only come in from a marathon on his laptop about an hour before. I went to sit on the veranda looking out over the backyard. The poui tree was full with fresh green leaves. It would flower in June and the ground would be covered with gold petals. Since we moved to this house I've looked forward to the transformation this tree makes to our yard once a year. That morning, after taking a few deep breaths, I sat upright with my feet firmly pressed against the floor which was damp. It was a stretch to imagine roots growing out of my feet through the floor and piercing the earth beneath; but I faithfully followed Nasrine's suggestions. The floorboards on the veranda squeak a bit when we walk on them because they have shrunk. I told Arnold we should get them repaired because someone could slip on them and fall when they're damp. He'd agreed but I'm sure he has forgotten since he's mired in his melancholic world. Just then I heard the boards squeak followed by a thud. I opened my eyes and there was Arnold on the floor in his pyjamas with a look of surprise on his face.

"Are you okay?"

"Yeah. The floor is slippery."

"We need to get it fixed to keep the area dry."

"Yeah, I guess so. Sorry I disturbed you."

"That's okay; I should have gone into the garden." I stood up and he quickly picked up his cell phone which had fallen. He examined it closely, gently dusted it off with his hand, rubbed it against his chest, then went back into the house.

I walked down the steps towards the bench under the poui tree and sat. The birds fussed and flew off from the tree when I approached. They chorused their displeasure from their perch on branches of the mango tree close by. I closed my eyes and placed my feet firmly on the ground. I imagined two thick roots sprouting from my soles and piercing the earth. I leaned against the tree, breathed deeply and ordered my muscles to relax. I began to repeat the mantra slowly, like a litany. The bird calls were insistent and I began to follow their conversations. The bullfinch was the loudest. I imagined a pair perched on a branch of the poui tree, the male puffing out his chest, grey feathers sticking out and his wings held slightly away from his body. He was making short sharp trills followed by a *coo-roo*, confusing his mate about his intentions. She responded with a trill followed by a soft *ork*. He trilled sharply again; I understood why and what he said. He was angry.

"Who she think she is coming here so early, interfering with the nest building?" His mate cooed and orked gently; she was trying to placate him.

"Don't fret; the nest almost done now, and besides, she does put seeds in the feeder for us so we always have food; *coo-roo*, don't fret."

I smiled, and I was elated because I knew that if I could understand birdsong, getting to a state of enlightened bliss couldn't be far away. I repeated the mantra with fervour and each chant was echoed by a plaintive cooing from a mourning dove in the hedge close by.

The cooing sounds took me back to the time when we first moved to this house. Arnold and I had been married for about a year and we found this place by accident after a few months of looking around. We had checked the advertisements in the papers regularly but the places we had seen were either too cramped or didn't have enough light or yard space or were too expensive for our budget. We had resigned ourselves to renting indefinitely when one morning we had gone to the beach and as we walked along the public access path, we saw a 'House for Sale' sign midway along, with an arrow pointing to a track. Without a word, we both turned and walked along the path. In a grove on a slight rise and surrounded by trees, we saw the cottage. It was quaint, painted in bright colours, with a veranda along the front and running the length of the house on the side facing the sea. Three steps led up to the veranda at the front. There was fretwork around the edge of the roof and running the length of the veranda. A woman was sitting in a rocking chair at one end of the veranda. She stood up when she saw us approaching.

"You come to see the house?" she called out as she moved to open the gate. We walked up the steps and introduced ourselves, apologizing for disturbing her.

"What you think I put the sign there for? You not disturbing me. I don't have a phone so you would have to come." She showed us around the house. The veranda was wide and I could see myself sitting there on an evening after work, reading or just enjoying the breeze. The front door opened on to a drawing room with jalousie windows at the front and along the sides. It was a cool, inviting room. I knew Arnold liked it because he muttered "Umm hmm" every now and then as a feature caught his eye. A short passageway led from the drawing room. It opened out on one side to a kitchen with an old stone hearth with three cooking pits and iron grilles fitted at the top of each. A kettle sat on one side of the grilles. It was an old-fashioned set-up but there was space next to it for a stove. On the opposite side of the corridor there was a dining room with windows that looked out over the side veranda and the sea. A round, brightly painted green table sat in the centre of the room and matching colour chairs with woven cane seats were pushed in neatly around it. In the centre of the table was a crocheted cloth with a vase full of pink and red ginger lilies.

"These come from my garden," Mrs Isidore said. "If you look, you will see I have all kind of flower growing there." She pointed towards the jalousie windows and the garden. "Look, you see the poui tree out there? When it flowering people does stop to look at it and the tourist does take pictures." There was a bench under the poui tree; it didn't have a backrest because the shape of the trunk formed a natural support. The branches were laden with fresh green leaves which Mrs Isidore said meant a full blossoming in mid-year. Further down the passage, there were two bedrooms on the left and a bathroom and storage area with built-in cupboards on the right. I glanced at them but the garden and poui tree had already convinced me that this was the ideal place for us. When we walked back through the front room, Mrs Isidore led us round to the side veranda. At the end of it a gate opened on to steps leading to the garden. I sat for a while under the poui tree and I could already see it ablaze with golden blooms. Mrs Isidore walked down the path with us and pulled up the "House for Sale" sign because she said the house was for us and she was certain she would see us again soon. So we bought the house.

I opened my eyes at the rush from the fluttering wings of the birds coming back to roost in the branches of the poui tree. The mantra had got lost in the flood of memories about our first visit to the house and I was nowhere near enlightenment. I heard the boards of the veranda creak and I looked up to see Arnold swiping the screen of his cell phone and reading. After a moment he looked up, saw me. He quickly put the phone in his pocket.

A few days ago, I discovered the reason for Arnold's seeming indifference and lack of attention. It happened by accident. I needed an envelope and I thought he might have some so I went to ask him for one. He wasn't at his desk but I knew he must have stepped away briefly because his computer was on. I started to look for an envelope and bumped into the computer which beeped twice so I knew it was receiving messages. The screen lighted up and the messaging tool showed up with a chat. I glanced at it and the message that had just come in startled me so I scrolled to the start of the exchange and read:

So have u told her? U said u would. Did u change your mind?

No, I haven't, but I will. Be patient.

OK, as long as U R not just saying that 2 put me off. I hope U R as happy as I am that we found each other again.

I began to figure out that the "her" the person was referring to must be me. I read Arnold's response.

The internet makes the world smaller. I'm glad you got in touch.

Well, U seemed distant at first so I had to be persistant.

She can't even spell, I thought.

Yes you were persistent.

He wrote the word correctly, tactfully indicating the spelling, I supposed. She went on.

I know what I'll do. I'm going 2 send U a poetry.

I would have laughed if I hadn't found the whole thing distasteful.

Oh, a poem, yes. That's nice.

The one U sent me was real nice. I like it a lot: "Roses are red, violets are blue, sugar is sweet . . ."

That's an old simple verse.

It don't matter. Simple, but nice. Thanks for the presents U sent by FedEx. I like them. When I got home from walking the dog, there was this package with a CD, Amici Forever. I'm sure U chose that one because the title represents us, right? I put it on right away and my favourite is the song "Whisper of Angels". It's as if I hear U speaking 2 me when I listen 2 it. I like the lines where she is singing "I was yours before the sun had warmed the earth, before rain kissed the ground" and where he sings "I'll be the whisper of Angels, I'll be the frost on your glass, I'll be your first, your last." I imagined you saying that.

I felt numb after reading this. There was a break and then the start of a new message. I guess that's the one that had come in when I heard the beep. I read on.

Thanks for the chocolates too. I love chocolates. Ta, and ta again. I'll enjoy, but if U meant what U said about looking forward 2 seeing me "face to face", ha, ha I noticed the underlining of that and tingled when I read Ur comment that I should understand that in every sense; LOL – I am, I am, and I can't wait, but don't send any more chocolates or U might be disappointed with the face 2 face.

Then there was an emoji with pouting red lips blowing kisses, followed by another with a throbbing heart. There was nothing further.

My head felt light and I had the sensation of being in a different space, another world, but the feeling wasn't one of bliss. How could he, I thought. He knew nothing about the Amici group until I bought the CD. He knows how much I like it, because I play it often and sit in the rocking chair on the veranda and listen while the wind breathes through the poui branches. I dropped heavily in his chair, rested my head against the back and looked up at the ceiling. I wondered how long this had been going on, and I concluded that his distance over the last two months wasn't the usual melancholy. It must have been because of this. I wasn't sure it was just an Internet Affair and thought I should find out. I leaned forward to search further just as Arnold walked in.

"What are you doing, Mavis?" Looks like it's Mavis now for keeps, I thought.

"Reading your love story, as you can see. I came to look for an envelope but found this instead. I suppose you were in this love exchange before you stepped away."

"How could you?"

"How could I not, when it is here in black and white staring me in the face? My face; clearly not the face to face you seem to be yearning for. No wonder you've been calling me Mavis."

"This is private, Mavis."

"Private and wrong. It's adulterous. How long has this been going on, Arnold?"

He winced. "Don't make it sound like that. She isn't even here."

"Lucky for you because if she were you would have had your face to face already. I didn't know I married a cheat."

He grimaced. "I'm not a cheat . . ."

"You aren't? Do you think because it's on the internet it's okay? It's as bad or worse if you've been surfing the net to make connections. And you're always on your cell phone and holding on to it for dear life. Now I understand why. How could you send her my favourite CD? And love poems too, I see. You've never sent me any. She can't even spell, for heaven's sake. Who and where is she?"

"Okay, Mavis. This isn't as bad as you think. It's an old girlfriend from college days. A mutual friend sent her my email and she got in touch. Things happened from there . . ."

"I'll say they have. You're sending her gifts. How could you send her the Amici CD? Now you've spoiled it for me totally."

"I'm sorry, Mavis. I didn't mean for this to happen. It just did."

"You must have encouraged it, Arnold. Otherwise you would not be writing and doing things that lovers say and do."

"I haven't seen her in years, Mavis."

"But here you are, carrying on a love affair with her on the net."

"It's lonely here and you're always meditating. You're in a world of your own that I can't enter. You talk on the phone about these things with your friends. What about Charles, your old boyfriend? He calls sometimes to talk about meditation and I'm left out."

"Bollocks, Arnold! And you know it. I haven't heard from Charles in a long while."

"Well, he called just yesterday when you were out to say that he's coming and he'd like to drop by for a visit."

"And you were so caught up in your online romance you didn't tell me."

"I forgot. I'm telling you now."

"You know Charles is just a friend, so don't use him as an excuse for your infidelity."

"I wasn't."

"This can't go on, Arnold, You have to decide. I can't live with someone I can't trust."

"What do you want me to do?"

"You're asking me? Are you going to continue with this? I can't stay with you if you are." He looked at me with a surprised expression then looked away quickly. I wondered what he expected me to say. I got up. He leaned forward and closed the lid of the laptop.

"That won't make this go away," I told him. He opened his mouth, started to say something, stopped and shook his head.

I left and went into the garden to sit on the bench under the poui tree. It was evening and the birds were coming in to roost. I thought I heard the bullfinch couple with their *coo-roos* and soft *orks*, comforting each other. They have each other for life, I thought. They will build their nest, have a brood this year, perhaps another next year and they'll remain with each other till death. There's a lot we can learn from birds. It was still light but a full moon was rising. I could hear the waves rushing to shore in the distance. I leaned against the trunk of the poui and it seemed to be curved and more comfortable than I remembered. I closed my eyes and without thinking I began to repeat the mantra. I tried hard not to think about what had just happened. I imagined roots sprouting from my feet and the sound of the waves reminded me of the whisper of angels. I don't know how long I sat there. I heard the boards on the veranda creak and I opened my eyes to see Arnold leaning against the balustrade, looking out. It was dark, except for the moonlight dripping on the grass between the branches. It hadn't rained but my cheeks were wet.

It's been two days since I found out about Arnold and the person. I'm surprised that I don't feel anger or resentment towards him. When I went into the garden to meditate right after, I was hurt and angry but for the first time I had no thoughts and was unaware of my surroundings for about an hour. I think I fell asleep, but since then I've been feeling light-headed and somewhat upbeat, as though a load has been lifted off me. I suppose it's because I finally found out what was wrong between us. On the day after, Arnold avoided me. He spent hours on his laptop but did not go back after dinner. This morning, before he left, he handed me an envelope. I opened it and read the note he wrote just before I left to meet Rita for lunch. It was an apology.

> Dear Mav,
> What I did was stupid, and I'm sorry. Let's find that common place from which we can restart our relationship. I've deleted all the conversations on my laptop and stopped communicating with the person. That is over. We owe it to ourselves to make a go of it together.

I told Rita what had happened and about my meditation too. I asked her if not being aware of one's surroundings for an entire hour was the state she talked about. She said it was definitely not because a person can't mistake the feeling of transcendence. She said that the upbeat feeling I described was probably a manifestation of my desire to escape from the situation with Arnold. I'm thinking about that. I know I'm hurt and my trust in Arnold is shattered but even though he has apologized I'm not sure I want to get close and become vulnerable in case it happens again. Perhaps Rita is right. Perhaps I want to escape. I sit in the rocking chair on the veranda and look across the water to see if today, I can see the green flash of the sun when it sinks below the horizon because there isn't a cloud in sight and the sea is calm. I read over Arnold's note and realize that I don't even know the person's name, so I insert no name where he says he's stopped communicating with her. I notice too that he calls me Mav in the note, but even though he does so, he doesn't say he loves me, he doesn't sign the note and he doesn't promise not to do anything like this again. I suppose in his self-absorbed fashion he thinks that finding a common place to restart the relationship implies love renewed. I'm thinking I will need much more to get me back to the place he mentions.

The sun is about to set and it seems to move faster as it sinks below the horizon. I stare at it and as the last bit of the upper curve disappears, a bright green flash lights up the spot on the horizon. I'm elated because I've never seen it this bright before. I take it for a good omen. I walk down the steps into the garden towards the bench under the poui tree. The birds are coming in to roost and the bullfinch and his mate are perched on a branch right above the bench. They do not fly away when I sit down. I lean against the trunk; it's still warm from the afternoon sun and it seems to enfold me as I press my back against it. I can hear the susurration of the wind through the casuarinas lining the beach. A poui flower drops on my lap. I pick it up. It is bright yellow. I close my eyes, press my feet against the ground and lean my head against the tree. I imagine roots shooting from the soles of my feet into the ground. I make circles with my thumbs and index fingers and begin to repeat the mantra.

My roots curl around clumps of rich earth, spread across the yard and down towards the sand and the sea. I sink more comfortably into the warm trunk. A petal falls on my forehead. I focus on repeating the mantra. I'm not sure how long I've been doing this but now, I feel enveloped by the tree. Poui blossoms fall on my head and my face. Yellow-gold colour seeps into my eyelids. A delightful lassitude creeps over my body and my mind fills with a glowing light.

The wind breathes through my branches and I am showered with petals. I want to stay here forever. From a distance I hear Arnold calling. His voice disturbs me. I intone the mantra to block the sound of his voice. The faint sound of boards creaking wafts up to me and I know he is on the veranda. He's talking to someone. Their voices reach me through a fog.

"She's usually here at this time," Arnold says. "She either sits in this rocking chair or on the bench under the poui."

"Perhaps she went for a walk down the beach?" It is Charles. He has come to visit as promised.

"I don't think so, not this late. But you never know; Mav is unpredictable."

"Your garden is lovely. Just look at that poui tree. It's magnificent."

"It's Mav's favourite."

Footsteps come down the steps into the garden. They come close to the poui.

"Just look at those blossoms! I've never seen such an abundance of flowers."

"It's the first time I've seen so many. Mav will be delighted."

The wind picks up and rustles through my branches.

"Such a delicate perfume. I could stand here for hours with my arms outstretched, like this, absorbing the magic of this tree."

"Believe me, Charles, it isn't always like this. For most of the year it's just an ordinary tree with leaves."

"I wouldn't mind if it were only a stick in the ground if I knew that there's a moment when it transforms into this. Look, just look at this blossom, Arnold. Isn't it lovely? What an exquisite, perfect Florette."

Virgo

The night before her wedding they checked her horoscope in fun. Veronica said that on such an auspicious occasion it was worthwhile finding out what the stars had in store. They bought a copy of the *Trinidad Guardian*, which they knew, of all the regional papers, had the best horoscope section. Morella tossed the paper into a corner when Veronica appeared with it. "You can't be serious," she said. "What possible bearing could this fabricated astrological stuff have on my life?"

"Ha! You never can tell." Veronica laughed, gathering the strewn pages together. "You're Virgo, aren't you? This is what it says: *Neptune turns directly in your relationship sector and the power of his station may cast clouds over your love life. There is some joy and a bit of sorrow too. Be careful and keep a watch on your heart.*"

"See what I mean? Utter foolishness. Sorrow my foot! What does that old popular song say? 'Into each life some rain must fall . . .', something like that; but all ends well, right? Clouds send showers of blessings. That's my interpretation, so no more predictions that are written for every creature born under the sign of Virgo. I claim my unique destiny."

"And so you should," Veronica retorted. "We're rooting for you, girl."

They gathered in the church the next afternoon, to witness the start of Morella's unique destiny as Mrs Duplesis, wife of Theodore, dashing teacher of French to the fifth formers of the girls' school. They'd all had a crush on him at one stage or another, but Morella won out in the end. "Don't you think this is too hurried?" Veronica asked Jessica. "I'm happy for her but we've just finished sixth form with all the restrictions the nuns imposed. We should be having fun, don't you think? Marriage is serious business."

"That's what Morella wants. She'll have all the fun going off to live on a different island while we hang around here looking for jobs. She'll be okay."

Jessica and Veronica watched with a bit of envy as Morella aligned her future with Theodore's. They left the island soon after and life continued. Jessica got a job at one of the local banks and she was happy to move up the ranks and carve a career for herself as a banker.

One day, as she left work and rushed through the crowded main street, she saw Morella. She had got a bit plump but she strode with the same self-assured gait, her head thrown back defiantly, a posture that had sometimes got her into trouble with the nuns who thought she was being "insubordinate". She rushed across the street, heedless of the traffic to catch up with Morella.

"Jess, my goodness, how long it's been!" Morella spread her arms and hugged Jess in her expansive way. Jessica took a step backwards and looked Morella up and down with exaggerated inspection.

"My dear, you look perfectly peachy. Where on earth have you been, Mrs Duplesis?"

The smile left Morella's face. "I don't answer to that name anymore."

Jessica was surprised. "How come? What on earth happened?"

"A lot, but it's over." Morella's smile returned. "I have remarried, as you can see." She flashed her left hand towards Jessica, showing off a gold ring with a large diamond and another simple gold band below it.

"Mmm hmm; impressive. Your first ring was silver, wasn't it?"

"Yes, it was, and perhaps that's why things didn't last." She laughed.

"I see you have become superstitious. If I had said something like that to you before you went away, you would have told me off."

"Age makes us wiser, m'dear. I met a charming man in Toronto and he has remained charming, so I'm happy."

"None of this was mentioned in the article I read about you the other day. Your father put it in the weekend paper. You are now a top surgeon working miracles for many. I liked that article."

"An exaggeration. You know daddy. But I enjoy my work with Doctors Without Borders. We travel to many countries and work in poor communities to help needy people, especially children."

"That's great. But what on earth could have gone wrong with Theodore? And why didn't you write? I wondered about you."

"That doesn't matter now, does it? Look how we've picked up the threads as though we saw each other yesterday. I'm here for a while. One of these days let's meet for lunch and we can have a good laugh about our adolescent gaffes."

"So is Mr What's-His-Name . . . the Duplesis replacement . . . here with you?"

Morella smiled. "No, but Mr Lestrade calls all the time so it's as if he were here. That's the name now, so don't mention the other one again."

"Okay. Can't wait to hear about this. Morella, you always did have a flair for drama, you know."

"Nothing to do with drama. We'll talk later. See you soon."

They didn't have lunch because Morella called Jessica to say she had to leave on urgent business. Two years later she was back, and she called Jessica.

They sat on the back gallery at Jessica's house one afternoon. Morella looked frail and drawn and she asked Jessica for ginger tea instead of the Earl Grey Jessica had bought to celebrate the reunion.

"I tried to get Veronica to come along," Jessica said. "She had to go down south on business. She said she'll call you."

Morella nodded and sipped her tea. She breathed out a plume of smoke and flicked the ash from the end of her cigarette.

She said, "Jess, you wanted to know what happened. Since you asked, I'll tell you. You know I was an incurable romantic. I used to tell you all about the latest spicy Mills & Boon novels in the library. I was a sucker for romance." She chuckled. "When I met Theodore he seemed to fit the bill for the ideal person I wanted to spend my life with. Our courting was almost like the ones I'd read about in those novels too. He used to come to the house in the afternoons after school and we'd sit and listen to the Drifters, the Supremes, and Nat King Cole. We half-believed that we lived in that tinsel world extolled on vinyl.

You remember, Jess, TV in those days had only just come to us and we got one channel from five in the afternoon to ten at night. Theodore and I watched *Peyton Place, Days of Our Lives* and every silly show that fuelled our romance. I should have been more alert, but I was smitten. Any man who craves a bowl of cream of wheat after a long day of teaching must be strange. Anyway, once I discovered he liked it, I would have it ready, piping hot, waiting to be served to him as soon as he arrived. You probably remember; I used to tell you all about those episodes before I got married."

"We all knew you'd gone clean out of your head, girl." Jessica put an index finger on each temple, opened her eyes wide and rolled them round.

"Not as bad as that!" Morella laughed and had a protracted spasm of coughing.

"You okay?"

"Yeah, I'm fine." She stretched her arms above her head. Jessica noticed she had lost muscle tone. She took a long drag on her cigarette, exhaled in a series of smoke rings, then continued. "He insisted on getting married. My father thought we should wait but my parents were impressed with him." She smiled. "I could have spent all my time with him. That's how bewitched I was. So we went to Trinidad to be with his mother who had gone there and was living alone. He wanted to be there to help her." She stopped, opened her bag, took out a cigarette, lit it from the one she held and crushed the stub in the ashtray on the table. She inhaled, looking at Jessica out of the corner of her eye.

"Don't bother say anything, you hear? I know what the stats show."

She leaned back in her chair. The sunlight slanting through the wooden jalousie louvres accentuated the shadows beneath her eyes.

"His mother was a nice person. She made me feel welcome. She seemed to be happy to have her son near her. You know, she lasted just under two years after we got there. We hadn't planned to live in her house but when Theodore saw how difficult things were for her, he suggested it and she was happy to have us. That part of it was fine. Between part-time classes at the university, my teaching job at the primary school, getting home late most evenings, things became a bit stressful. Theodore had a full-time job teaching at one of the secondary schools and he was also taking part-time courses in theology at the seminary on the hill. He inevitably came home late as well, usually later than me." She pulled on her cigarette. "As if that wasn't strain enough, our relationship was fast becoming one."

She tilted her head and seemed to be in deep thought for a moment. She looked up at Jessica. "By the end of the day we were exhausted. At first, I used this as an excuse to try to understand what might be going on, but it became a pattern and I couldn't ignore it any longer." She smiled, drew in her breath sharply and looked out the window. She shook her head. "Can you believe that we had been married for two whole months and the marriage had not been consummated?"

"What you saying, girl? You joking." Morella laughed and ended up with another coughing fit. Jessica leaned forward, poured some more tea into her mug and handed it to her.

"You don't believe me." It was more a statement than a question. Jessica looked bewildered. She spread her palms upwards, in the most noncommittal gesture she could manage.

"I see that you don't. You know I wouldn't make up something like that, Jess." They sat in silence for a while. Morella leaned forward. "At first, it didn't seem to matter too much because we were both rushed. We cuddled, but he would say he was afraid his mother would hear us because the partition between the bedrooms was thin. He didn't want to disturb her with our sounds of delight. His words, not mine. For me it wasn't delight to be aroused and brought to the brink of ecstasy only to have someone say 'Shhh', turn away, fall asleep and snore." She shook her head when she saw the expression on Jessica's face.

"That's probably how I reacted the first time it happened. I put up with it at first because I believed . . . I knew he loved me and we were both under pressure. I let it go. After his mother died we had the house to ourselves and there was no need to worry about thin partitions, but nothing changed. I began to think there was something wrong with me. One morning in desperation I confided in our friend, Torero; you remember him, don't you? He was studying for the priesthood at the seminary. I remember our meeting as though it happened yesterday. We sat on a stone bench under a spreading flamboyant tree in the garden of the seminary. The petals were strewn across the grass. Torero stared at me in disbelief when I told him about this. Much the way you're looking at me now. I had to tell him twice before he said anything.

"He asked me whether Theo is gay.

"I said at first I'd wondered whether he might be but he's not. I told Torero I suspected that some psychological issue was the problem. He seemed afraid to commit himself for some reason. Torero asked me if nothing had happened. That was the difficult part to explain to him. I told Torero things happened up to a point. We made love but he just could not bring himself to have sex or let's say to complete the sexual act. I hadn't told anyone else before and had not even said it aloud to myself for fear my saying it would make it an indisputable fact. But, when Torero asked, I told him, and didn't need to mask it with all the euphemistic statements and excuses I'd made up to explain it to myself. He just couldn't conclude what he started. He never seemed able to. I was going to say he didn't seem to want to but that isn't true either. I think he did but there was something keeping him back."

She had another fit of coughing and took some deep breaths before continuing.

"Torero asked me if I was still a virgin and I said that I was, technically. You know Torero. He went on in his usual dramatic fashion. 'Jézi Kwi!' he said, then he must have remembered where he was because he asked forgiveness for calling out the Lord's name like that. Then he looked at me and said, 'So you're Virgo intacta!' He laughed when he said this. He repeated 'Virgo intacta' more than once, as though trying to digest its meaning. I didn't think it funny, but he was laughing as he said it. Then he reached out and held my hands and I broke down and cried. It was like letting out all the frustration, hurt and doubt I had bottled up. Torero put his arms around me and held me while I bawled. Then inexplicably, I started to laugh. I laughed and laughed and tears were streaming from my eyes. After that I felt relieved."

"Where is Torero now?" Jessica asked. "I haven't seen him in ages."

"He got ordained and went to Ghana to serve there for a while. The priesthood was his true calling. Perhaps it was for Theodore too, but with him life was always complicated. Anyway, Torero's coming back for good so I'm sure you will get to see him."

Jessica smiled; tried to change the subject. "Morella, do you remember how Torero got that name? The way he used to dance as though he were in a bullfight, stepping lightly and sweeping his arm as though holding a muleta? Do you remember the night of the sixth form party when Veronica, out of sheer mischief lunged at him just as he was doing this fancy little step and he was so startled he jumped aside and she burst out laughing and said, 'Fellas, fellas, look, I made him do a Veronica!' That was funny." Morella nodded, smiled, then went back to her story.

"Even though Torero was beginning his studies he seemed to know what to say to help me out of the funk I was in. After I calmed down, he took back his soaked handkerchief, folded it neatly in a square and repeated softly to himself, 'Virgo intacta.' I told him it was ironic, but I was Virgo in more senses than one. You know I don't believe in that astrology stuff, but it struck me that my sign is Virgo and I whispered, 'It's written in the stars that I should be so.' He smiled when I said that and told me I could get an annulment. I'd thought about that too, but decided to wait to see what Theodore would do. To be honest, back then I didn't have the will to do anything.

"Torero went on and on about how beautiful our wedding ceremony was, how lucky we were to have each other blah blah. Lucky, my foot! Everything after was wormwood. Funny thing is, I believed he loved me, but it was more platonic than romantic. He seemed to love some idea much more than me. It couldn't have been more than a month after Torero and I had that conversation than Theodore began acting in the most eccentric ways. He began using Latin to greet me. When we woke up in the morning he would hug me and say, 'Dominus vobiscum' and he'd do the same at odd times when we were at home together. He'd plant a kiss on my forehead and utter some blessing. I took these as signs. He was doing that to tell me something, to prepare me in the only way he knew how." She had another fit of coughing, sipped some tea and continued.

"I was getting more resentful by the day and could have hit him every time he came close, but I would just turn away. I eventually moved into his mother's room because I couldn't stand it anymore. It was more peaceful for me to be there than to lie in bed next to him. All the blessings he showered on me couldn't extinguish the fires he'd set raging in my veins."

She glanced at Jessica.

"So there you have it. That was the beginning of the end, although I think I always knew what the end would be. It was written in the stars."

Morella left and went back to Canada. She kept in touch with Jessica who knew from the emails Morella sent that the coughing fits she had were symptoms of something more serious. Torero returned to the island and he went to visit Jessica.

They talked about Morella and how worried they were because she had gone off on yet another project to some far-flung island in the Pacific where it was not possible for her to get the kind of help she needed to battle her illness. They got around to talking about her and Theodore.

"That stuff with Theodore was tough," Jessica said. "Torero, she sat right where you're sitting and told me about it. That marriage was a nightmare."

"I found it hard to take in too, Jess, but I guess I understood a little better after Theodore told me his story."

"You mean he actually had a story worth telling? Hmmm. I can tell from your tone that you empathized with him."

"Not quite. I did tell him he had given Morella a rough deal, but I understood how things turned out the way they did eventually."

"Hmmm. Some story that must have been!"

"Yes. And if you heard him tell it you would probably understand too. When he came up to the seminary to study after the marriage was annulled, I asked him about it. At first, he didn't want to speak of it, but one evening before vespers I was sitting under the flamboyant tree in the garden and he plunked himself on the bench next to me, right where Morella had sat when she poured her heart out. Jess, I know you're sympathetic to Morella; we both are; but Theodore's story is fascinating."

"Okay, then tell me. Can't wait to hear it."

"He sat quietly on the stone bench for a long while, then he turned to me. This is his version. He said, 'I suppose you resent me because of Morella, don't you?'

"'Not really. I've been more bewildered than resentful because I can't understand why you decided to marry her in the first place. She went through a very bad time.' He stood up, kicked at some of the fallen petals, then sat again abruptly.

"'Torero, you have to understand. I always wanted to be a priest. There was something about the mystery of the Eucharist that captured my imagination from the time I was small. I used to pretend saying mass with Keynote and Jo-Jo, my friends who lived on the same street. They used to come over to play after school. When my mother was outside washing or when she went out we would sneak into her room and use her dressing table as an altar. I would cut up roti skins into small round pieces for communion and I would raid some of the VP Rich Ruby wine from a bottle she kept for special occasions. So we would have our mass.'

"Jess, I wasn't sure he wanted to tell me his story. He would look up at me and then look down quickly at his shoes. He did that often while he talked so I knew he was uncomfortable, but he went on with it. I'm telling you in his own words as best as I can remember. This is what he said:

"'I knew most of the Latin phrases and I liked to turn towards Jo-Jo and Keynote with my mother's skirt flowing from my shoulders just like a chasuble and I would spread my arms and give a blessing, the Latin one I knew best. Jo-Jo and Keynote would crack up sometimes, but I would not give them communion unless they gave a proper response. They liked the wine and roti so they would eventually say something even though it wasn't the right thing. That didn't matter. It was play-acting. It all ended on the day when we had too much wine and were lolling about singing Kitchener's old hit – I can't remember the title but it had the line "Kitch, come go to bed, I got a small comb to scratch you head."

Keynote was singing that line in falsetto when we looked up and saw my mother standing in the doorway, arms akimbo and thunder on her face.

"'I don't know how Jo-Jo and Keynote got out of there so fast. My mother was not amused. She scolded me roundly as she watched me clean up the room. "So Mr Priest, Bishop and Pope Duplesis. Is so you making joke with God business? And who tell you to take de wine, eh? Who give you permission? What happen to you? Because you don't see a man in dis house it don't mean it don't have a boss, you hear? I is de boss so watch youself and behave before I cut yuh tail. You ent too big for me to do dat yuh hear? Watch yuhself."

"'I realized later on that it must have been difficult for her to raise me on her own, to find the fees for secondary school, uniforms, books, bus fare, everything. She was my mother and father rolled into one because I rarely saw my father. I didn't like to go to his house because it was always uncomfortable. His children would look at me as though I had come from Mars and his wife always made me wait on the doorstep until he came to let me in. Sometimes he seemed uncomfortable too and I eventually told my mother I would not go there anymore. I suppose my father's absence must have influenced my choices in some way. When I left school, I applied to become a priest but they turned me down. They sent me a polite letter which gave as a reason the circumstances of my birth. I was illegitimate and they said they were not enrolling illegitimate boys into the priesthood. I was disappointed and I had no choice but to accept that and move on with my life. You know most of the rest of the story, of how I met Morella. You were a part of that group. At one time I thought you liked Morella too, but she said you were just good friends.

"'You know Morella is a great dancer. I used to dance with her almost exclusively at those parties we used to have. Before I knew it, I fell in love with her and I impulsively asked her to marry me because I didn't think I had any future in the church. My mother was pleased. I think she was relieved because she had seen how disappointed I was when the rejection letter came. She'd held it up disdainfully by one corner as she said, "Eh, eh, is so the church doing its business now? Since when God does show prejudice, eh? If is so they stop I ain't going to church." She actually stopped for a while.

"'Morella and I were frazzled from all the stuff we were doing. I've thought about this over and over and, for the life of me, I can't explain why things turned out the way they did.'

"Jess, I asked Theo whether he had a problem with his sexuality. I began to ask him if he was gay but he chimed in before I could complete my sentence. He was upset with me. I could tell from his tone of voice: 'I'm not gay! And I don't have an explanation for what happened. Morella asked me more than once. That wasn't it. But what explanation was there?'

"He was really uncomfortable telling me all this, Jess. He stood up abruptly, crushed some petals underfoot, sighed, sat down and continued.

"'I loved Morella, Torero, but I just couldn't bring myself to take our lovemaking to the ultimate conclusion. I was tormented. Every day I set out with resolve to end my wretched vacillation but when it got to the point I failed again and again. I sensed her frustration and worry. I felt horrible when she asked "Theo, is it me?" I would hasten to reassure her, but I didn't have any reason to give that she could accept because it was beyond my own understanding. I didn't deserve her and I shouldn't have married, but at the time I didn't know I would have a problem. It just happened. She knew I wasn't impotent so I guess she believed I was rejecting her.'

"I asked Theodore if he told his mother. He said he didn't, but she seemed to know something. He said Morella must have told her because she asked him about it indirectly.

"'One day she called me into her room and cleared a space on her bed for me to sit. She said, "Theo, dis pain not going away. Like it getting worse every day." I told her she needed to rest and take her medication. She said, "I trying; I just worry I ent go be here to see my granchile." I shifted uncomfortably because she was edging into territory I didn't want to discuss. She looked at me for a while before she went on, "How come you and Ella taking so long to try for a baby? Ella tell me you practising natural birth control. What is dat?" Torero, I breathed a sigh of relief. I thought I was off the hook for a while. I thought perhaps Morella had not confided fully in her. My relief was short-lived. She pulled herself up against the pillows, closed her eyes and said, "Theo, you ent see what happenin to Ella? She tell me, but I can't believe that one whole year pass since you marry and you living like brother and sister. Why you doing Ella that? What happen to you?"

"'There was nothing I could say that made sense. She sat up and looked at me. "Ent you get over that priest foolishness? Is dat you still have in you head? Ent they tell you you kyan be a priest? How you can do dat to Ella, Theo?" I told her I loved Morella but she hissed through her teeth in a drawn out steeeups and turned away. "You say you love her but how she go know it if you does turn your back on her, eh? How she go know it? Dis is the life you choose. It ent have no future for you in de church, you know dat. Think 'bout the nice children you and Ella can have."

"'I was embarrassed that she knew about the situation and there was nothing I could say to explain it or assure her that there would soon be a grandchild. Her talk helped me to see how selfish I was, but I had to tell her that I would try so as not to add to the torment she was already suffering. She died some months later. I thought Morella was going to divorce me, but she didn't and then the bishop told me the rules had changed.

"'One day I made reservations for dinner at a good restaurant and suggested to Morella that we should get an annulment. She looked at me intently while I blurted out the prepared speech that sounded trite to my own ears. "Why did you marry me?" she asked. I told her I still loved her, that I always would and I wanted us to be friends always. She slipped the wedding ring off her finger, placed it on my bread plate, smiled at me and said, "I would like some champagne. A good one. We should celebrate your liberation." That was it. She moved out even though I told her she could have the house. I eventually donated it to the church. You know the rest. You must believe me, Torero, when I tell you how much I regret what happened. I feel a strong guilt that even my vocation won't erase.'

"That's his version, Jess."

Three months later Morella was back. They were in the church again. It was a moving ceremony. Jessica and Veronica were there as they had been at her wedding. The scene was similar to the one years before except for the solitary box that took up space where Morella and Theodore had stood. Torero swung the censer, sending up waves of fragrant incense around the coffin. Theodore followed closely behind, head bowed. The church had changed a bit too. The plain walls were now covered with the local artist's frescoes and the marble main altar had been moved forward allowing for the celebrant to face the congregation. The extravagant flower arrangements, the long-stemmed lilies that had seemed to lean out of the vases towards them in joyous exuberance were now replaced by carefully sculpted circular arrangements with anthurium lilies and forget-me-nots nestled in green foliage.

Torero was superb. His voice choked with emotion now and then as he recalled the carefree school days, the parties, Morella's generosity, giving her time and talent to serve with Doctors Without Borders. He skipped the Duplesis episode, but there Theodore was, large as life, robed in a chasuble that enfolded his body more symmetrically than his mother's skirt must have done. He sat motionless, head tilted slightly, as he listened to Torero's oration. His expression was inscrutable. He seemed impassive, but at the end, as they came forward for the commendation, Torero gave him the sprinkler and he walked around the coffin liberally dousing it with holy water. He read the final prayer with an even tone and when he turned at the end, a shaft of sunlight caught a glint on his cheek. He raised his arms and with tremulous voice intoned, "Dominus Vobiscum."

Savi's Trial

"I'm Savitree. Please have a seat. How can I help?"

"How can I help you?" I repeated louder because he was standing there staring at me as though he was in some sort of trance. Mr Blenman, a senior partner in the firm, had insisted that I see this Mr Gervais Singh, even though I had reminded him that I would be away on holiday and did not want to take on any new assignments. I had been clearing my desk and looking forward to starting my holiday the following day. I held out my hand.

"Oh, sorry," Mr Singh said. He shook my hand hastily and lowered himself to the edge of the chair, leaning forward and plunking his elbows on my desk, seeming unable to shift his gaze from my face. "Sorry, I didn't mean to stare."

"That's okay. He seemed agitated and I tried to put him at ease. "What can I do for you?"

"I don't know how to begin, but I need some legal advice." He shook his head as though trying to deny something or get rid of a memory. "This has been a horrible day. I got a call from the hospital to say that my mother had been admitted. When I got there she was in the Intensive Care Unit with a tube coming out of her mouth and an intravenous hook-up. The doctor said she had ingested something that made her violently ill. My father had called the paramedics because she had been vomiting blood. I thought this was related to her cancer, but the doctor said he thought she may have ingested poison. They will let us know tomorrow whether they have to do surgery because of possible damage to her stomach."

"This must be worrying for you and your father; but how can I help?"

"I'm worried. He couldn't stop crying and kept saying, 'It's my fault, it's my fault', over and over. The paramedics said his behaviour was unusual and they mentioned having to report it. If they do, I expect the police may want to question my father at some point. Earlier this year, my mother was diagnosed with cancer and she has refused conventional treatment. She has been taking some herbal concoctions but they have never made her ill. She's lost a lot of weight and she told us to let her be. She said if this is how she is meant to die that's how she'll die. It's been tough watching her get weaker but she's strong-minded."

I wasn't sure why he thought it necessary to give me all these details.

"So what's the problem with your father?" I probably sounded a bit irritated, because he glanced at me and quickly looked away.

"We thought that perhaps a certain combination of the herbs might have caused the problem or that my mother used too much of one thing or combined some in error. But the doctors ruled that out. They said they found a trace of poison in the tests they ran and that may be responsible." He shook his head again. "She's in a bad way but I'm hoping she'll pull through."

"So, the herbs were tainted with poison . . . by mistake?"

"No. My father told me that he and my mother had discussed her situation and she told him she didn't want to get to a stage where she was totally useless in a bed, wasting away. He said they agreed that he would help her to take something that would let her go quickly and painlessly. She's suffered a lot from the cancer already – it was at an advanced stage when she was diagnosed." He paused and glanced at me again, then continued when I was silent. "At first he said he wasn't sure what happened. Then he said he had slipped a couple drops of something into her tea to ease her pain, but she had just a sip before she started to be sick. The cup was still full almost to the brim when I checked at home before coming here. Perhaps she got ill from an accumulation of other things she's been eating – The bitter cassava or the brown rice?" He was talking softly, to himself. He looked up at me and said, "I don't know." He pressed his knuckles into his eyes, sighed, then went on. "He said he told the paramedics he put something in her tea and I guess that raised a red flag. I'm worried, that's why I've come." His voice cracked. "You know what will happen if my mother dies."

"Yes, that's tough."

"My father loves my mother. He could only have done something if she wanted him to do it and if he thought it would help. I'm not even sure that he put anything in the tea apart from the saccharine drops she uses or if he put in anything at all. Maybe he just said that."

"Could be. But you don't know what happened, so if I were you I wouldn't jump to the conclusion that he and your mother had tried euthanasia. I know it's an offence here, but there's nothing concrete to suggest . . ."

"I know, I know, but I'm worried and I need to talk with someone legal." He paused briefly then continued. "All this unfolded this morning and I'm not sure what the paramedics . . ." He stopped abruptly and looked up at me. "I threw out the cup of tea when I went home."

"Where is your father now?"

"He's at the hospital, sitting with my mother in the ICU. He says he won't leave until she can speak to him but that may not happen for a while. I'll go there later and take him home. Can you speak with him?"

"Do you have any idea what might have been in the tea?"

"No. I don't. It didn't smell funny or anything. I don't even believe he put anything in. Maybe just the saccharine. He's forgetting things these days. It may have been the saccharine."

"So now we won't know because you threw out the tea."

"Yes, and I washed up."

"Do you have siblings?"

"No, I'm an only child. I had a sister who died soon after birth. My parents live in Belvedere, in the country; it's an easy drive but my father will stay with me tonight. I can bring him in the morning if you wish."

"I won't be in tomorrow. Was there anyone else in the house when this happened?"

"No. Someone usually goes in to help during the day, but she wasn't there when this happened."

"Okay, I'll speak with your father if you think it will help, but it's too late now and I'm away on holiday from tomorrow. I'll have to let Mr Blenman know about this. If nothing happens while I'm away, I can meet with your father when I get back. I'll need some contact information."

He handed me a card from a small case he pulled from his pocket. "Call me any time" he said. "And thank you." He held on to my hand a little longer than I thought necessary. I walked to the door and opened it.

"I wouldn't worry too much at this stage. Just think about helping your mother at this point."

"Thanks a heap. I appreciate this," he said as he reached out and placed his hand over mine on the doorknob. He was clearly grateful. I pulled my hand away gently and closed the door.

As I expected, nothing happened while I was away, but I followed up on my promise to meet with Mr Singh. I called him to get an update on his mother's condition and to arrange an interview with his father.

"We could meet over dinner," he said. "Is this evening okay?"

"That's fine. How about Carib Spice? Or perhaps Chinese Specialties if you prefer that. They're both centrally located and close enough."

"Carib Spice is fine. See you at 6:30?"

He was waiting on the sidewalk when I got there.

"Something about you . . ." He smiled as he opened the door. "I think my mother will like you instantly." The smell of fried onions and baked bread filled the room. We found a table for two in an alcove.

"Then I must meet her," I said, shrugging off my jacket. I thought it time that a case should be made for female lawyers to vary their wardrobe in court. The heat could be unbearable.

"I'm going to the hospital to see her after dinner. Would you like to come with me? My father will be there so you may have a chance to speak with him."

"Has he said anything more?"

"No. Every now and then he repeats that it's his fault and he holds her hand and whispers in her ear. I can't always hear what he says but

I've picked up the odd words, 'forgive' and 'pain'. The doctors say she is pulling out of this. We expect the best."

"Good, then. What she has to say will help." I hardly noticed what I ate as I listened attentively to the snatches of his life's story he shared.

"I got a scholarship to go to university. At first, my mother didn't want me to leave home. She was overprotective and she would often say she didn't want to lose me. I couldn't understand this but my father said it was because my sister had died as a baby and I was all they had. Eventually I persuaded her that I would be fine staying in the students' residence and I promised to return to visit during every holiday." I thought him intense, the way he leaned forward, looking directly into my eyes as he spoke. That was slightly disturbing but, at the same time, engaging. By the time we walked out of the restaurant we were laughing and sharing quips like good friends.

Mr Singh had his back to the door when we entered the room. He was leaning forward and speaking softly to his wife who was looking up at him but obviously couldn't speak because a tube hung from the corner of her mouth. Gervais cleared his throat and Mr Singh turned around.

"Is you son. I glad to see you." Gervais walked over to the bed and touched his mother's hand. "How you feeling, Ma?"

She looked up at him and blinked once.

"You see? She getting better. She know is you. Who you bring?" He peered at me over Gervais's shoulder.

"This is Miss King, Pa. She is the lawyer I told you about."

He leaned forward, squinting, and extended his hand. "Nice to meet you, Miss." He clasped my hand, peering at me through narrowed eyes.

"Miss King is the lawyer I asked to come and speak with you just in case."

"Yes, yes. You want to sit, Miss?" He motioned me to the chair next to the bed where he had been sitting.

"How Ma doing?"

"Doctor say she doing well. He say the tube will come out tomorrow."

"Perhaps it's better for us to speak outside the room," I said.

"Good idea," Gervais said. He leaned forward and touched his mother's hand gently. She turned her head and looked at me where I sat close to her bed. She blinked twice, and her gaze shifted quickly from my face to her son's face, then to Mr Singh's. There was a gurgling sound in her throat as though she wanted to cough or speak. Mr Singh rushed towards the door, saying, "I go call the nurse."

Gervais leaned over his mother. "Is all right, Ma. Is all right," he whispered.

"Please wait outside." The nurse brushed past and bent over Mrs Singh.

We stood in the corridor beside the door of the room. Mr Singh kept looking into the room through the square aperture in the door where a pane of glass must have been at one time.

"I don know what happen to Minna," he muttered. "Look, Nurse coming." He moved away from the door.

"She's okay," the nurse said. "Her blood pressure is slightly elevated and her pulse rate is a tad too fast but she's okay. Perhaps it's better if we limit the number of visitors this evening."

"You stay, Pa. I'll walk Miss King to the car park. I'll come back to take you home, and we can go to her office tomorrow morning." He turned to me. "Is that okay with you, Savi?"

"That's fine," I said, noting that he had dropped the "Miss King" and used the diminutive form of my name. Mr Singh pushed the door open to go back into the room.

"Nice to meet you, Miss King. We will talk tomorrow."

"Ma looked really agitated in there," Gervais said. "At what time tomorrow would you like to meet?" he asked.

I found my car keys and unlocked the door.

"I have an appointment at three, so if we meet just before noon, that will give us some time to get your father's story." He leaned forward, kissed my cheek and before I could say anything he opened the door quickly. "See you tomorrow, then."

I drove off feeling somewhat confused but strangely not offended and thinking that it was perhaps a proper culmination to the evening. I felt a level of comfort with him that was unusual for new acquaintances.

I met with Mr Singh and Gervais as we had arranged, but he wasn't much help because he couldn't remember if he had put anything in his wife's tea. He was stressed and this made him distracted and confused. We bought lunch in the hospital cafeteria and sat outside at a table under a flowering flamboyant tree.

Mr Singh placed a cold, trembling hand on mine. I tried to reassure him. "Don't worry, Mr Singh. I'm sure things will work out fine. If the police find some reason to pursue this, I will defend you."

He looked at me and said, "You remind me of how Minna did look when we marry."

Gervais chuckled. "That's a good omen, then," he said.

Mr Singh looked at me across the table. He covered his eyes with his hands and sighed deeply.

"It's going to be okay, Pa," Gervais said. "Not to worry."

"Is Minna I worrying 'bout, Vais. She suffer so much already, first with the baby girl and always tinking bout what happen to she. Then she get de cancer and that put suffering pon suffering."

"What did happen to her, Pa? Why is Ma blaming herself?"

"We ain know wha happen to duh chile, Vais. Is lose we lose she. She disappear from duh cradle one morning jus' so. Is you one dat left."

Gervais seemed stunned. "Why you never tell me that before, Pa?"

"Minna say it better if you don know. She say if we tell you, you will have a weight to carry and she din want you grow up wid anyting so on your mind. You and de lil girl was twins, Vais."

Gervais stared at his father, then he looked at me, his mouth open. This information given in a casual way by Mr Singh clearly troubled him. Mr Singh continued as though eager to unburden himself of a weight he had carried for too long.

"I 'member duh morning clear like was yesterday. Minna did go down by duh jetty to buy fish and I was in duh back garden. You an you sister was in duh big wicker basket we keep you in when we was outside. I hear Dulcie call out as she passin to go to work. She use to hail Minna to give she duh latest gossip. I tell she Minna out and I roun duh back. She say she will pass back later and I hear duh gate close. I go roun duh corner to pick some coreilli for Minna to cook. I wasn gone long den I hear Minna cry out. 'Raffie,' she shout. 'Where duh baby? Where duh lil girl?' When I look was only you in duh basket, Vais. I run out, go up and down duh road, I ask Miss Hettie by duh corner if she see somebody pass wif a baby or a bundle. She say she ain't see nuffing. It don have nobody else in duh street. I go back in duh house and Minna bawlin."

"But, Pa, you didn't go to the police?"

"Vais, children – girl-children was disappearin in duh place dat time. It was like a malady. One story was bout a father dey say trow way he girl chile in duh river because him did want a boy. Up duh road from where we was living, Vashti lil girl disappear and dey say is Vashti husband do something wid she. Ah was fraid to go to duh police. Dey would say is me do something with duh chile. Whole week I look for she. When we don find she we pack up and go back to Belvedere. Minna never get over it. I sure is dat give she de cancer."

I thought about his account of the disappearance of the child and the reason he gave for not telling Gervais the truth before. The story bothered me. I knew I would have to speak with Mrs Singh not just about her illness but about the information Mr Singh had just given. I wondered why Mr Singh chose this moment to tell his son about this event that had happened long ago. He seemed to remember the details well. Gervais had said he was forgetful. I wondered what he was thinking about his father's revelation and I asked him as he walked me to my car.

He was silent for a long while, then he said, "The thought that I have a sister, a twin who is possibly alive somewhere fills me with anxiety and longing at the same time. My mother was probably right because if I'd known before now, I would have started a search a long time ago. When this is all over, I'll do just that."

He held my arm as he opened the door and helped me in. "Shall we meet later? Dinner, perhaps?"

"Perhaps we shouldn't. I need to maintain professional distance in the event that there is a case and I have to defend your father."

"You just said it. It's my father you'd be defending, not me. That shouldn't matter, should it?"

I put the key in the ignition and started the car.

"It shouldn't in theory, but I think it best to be cautious. We'll see how things work out after that."

"Just so you know, I plan to be around – and not as a client. I hope you will let me." He leaned through the window, kissed my cheek, turned abruptly and walked away.

I felt uneasy. I needed to clear my head, to restore equilibrium to the situation and my own feelings which were drawn towards this stranger. I drove in the direction of my parents' house.

⁓ℐ

"You look tired, Savi. What's up?"

"It's a situation with a client – I should say possible client. There aren't any charges, but the son came to see me. I haven't been able to pin down the full story yet. The father is distracted by his wife's illness and he hasn't been able to say definitively what, if anything, he put in her tea. The tests showed a trace of poison although the son said he doesn't believe his father would have done anything to hurt his mother. He thinks he put the usual saccharine in her tea."

My father looked at me over the rim of his glasses, one eyebrow raised quizzically. "I'm sure you'll be able to handle it, if it gets to trial, Savi. I have confidence in my girl." He was a retired judge and he always made my cases seem simpler than I imagined them.

"I'm hoping it won't get to that, but I'd like to have an opportunity to speak with Mrs Singh. She's recovering from the effects of what may be poisoned tea. Their son, Gervais, is rather nice but he's too close to the situation to be objective. There isn't any need to pursue this now, but I told Gervais I would meet his parents and help with advice."

"Hmm . . . do I sense a particular interest?" He folded the newspaper and looked at me directly, one eyebrow still raised.

"We've had some meetings, dinner, lunch. I enjoy his company. There's an openness about him that I like. I think you'd like him and he's the sort of person Mama would have liked too. I miss her, mostly at times like this, you know."

"Me too, but you must be comforted in knowing that her leaving us meant freedom from pain. You were her sunlight and she spoiled you."

"Hah! I'm no worse off for that, am I?" I went over and sat beside him on the sofa. "Something Mr Singh said today nags me. He said his son's twin disappeared when they were small. He seems to think that Mrs Singh's illness is a result of her anguish over the loss of the girl. She was never able to get over it. He told Gervais about it during lunch and it was the first time Gervais had heard that story. Until now he believed his sister had died from some illness in infancy. I don't know why he chose to tell this story out of the blue." I felt my father's arm stiffen slightly under my touch.

"Yes, that's odd."

"Dad . . ." I waited a long while before I could ask him what I wanted to know.

"What is it?"

"I know I was adopted . . ." My voice trailed off.

"Yes, Savi, you were; but you're our very own. We loved you from the moment we saw you. Your mother was devastated when we discovered she could not have a baby so we decided to adopt. The agency did not have small babies at the time, mostly older children, and your mother wanted a baby. Our helper told us of two women who were about to put their babies up for adoption and we agreed to take you in as a foster child first. We made the arrangements and she brought you to us one day. You stole our hearts there and then."

"Which woman, Dad? Do you know which woman I came from?"

"No. Our helper offered to arrange a meeting, but your mother preferred not to meet the woman to avoid complications. I wanted your mother to be happy and went along with her decision."

"Can we find the helper?"

"Savi, she died years ago. I'm not even sure of the name of the person involved. I can't recall."

"What if it was the Singhs?" I had always thought that I would be able to trace my birth parents if I chose to, but until this moment I had not wanted to do so.

"Savi, I'm sorry. I should have followed this in the official way. We were just so happy to have you. I never imagined this could become complicated."

"What was the name of the baby she brought? I could ask the Singhs the name of the little girl they lost and that would let us know."

"We didn't have a name and your mother didn't want to know. She only wanted to receive you and to go through the motions of taking care of a baby as though she had given birth to it. So we selected your name that same day, then went through the process of registration, baptism and so on. Where did the Singhs live?"

"In Belvedere."

"Well, I'm sure the possibility of any link with the Singhs is remote because our helper never moved from this community. I wouldn't give it another thought."

I remembered after I left that Mr Singh had said they moved to Belvedere after the child went missing. The idea that there might be even the remotest possibility of a link with the Singhs troubled me.

It was a week before I could bring myself to face Gervais and his father again. I resolutely refused to pick up the phone on the many occasions he called and I never returned the calls. One afternoon I finally decided to go to the hospital unannounced to speak with Mr Singh and, hopefully, Mrs Singh. I pushed open the door to the room. Mrs Singh was sitting up against a bank of pillows, looking frail. Mr Singh was sitting on one side of the bed and Gervais was standing on the other side. Both had their backs to the door and each one was affectionately holding a hand of Mrs Singh and leaning towards her as she seemed to be saying something to them through laboured breathing. Mrs Singh looked towards the door when I walked in. Her eyes opened wide, her lips moved and Gervais turned sharply towards me. He came quickly to my side.

"Savi, where have you been? I've been calling you all week. My mother wanted to see you. Now she has fluid on her lungs and she can hardly breathe."

His father's voice from the bedside interrupted. "Call the nurse, Vais, call the nurse."

I walked over to the bedside. Mrs Singh looked up at me, smiled, said something as she stretched her arm towards me and tried to raise her body from the pillows that propped her up. I couldn't make out what she said as her breathing became more laboured.

"Vais, call the doctor, call the doctor." Mr Singh was beside himself.

The nurse came in and shooed us out of the room. The doctor pushed past us as we made our way out. Mr Singh walked around in the same small circle, wringing his hands while Gervais leaned against the wall chewing his bottom lip and glancing at me occasionally. There was nothing I could say to them in this moment, but the look on Mrs Singh's face when she saw me made me uneasy and I knew it would haunt me for a long time.

The doctor came out and shook his head. "I'm sorry," he said. "She's gone."

A thin wail escaped Mr Singh's lips as he ran past the doctor into the room. Gervais stood still against the wall, his head bent. I felt an indescribable sadness for him, for his father and for the feeling of loss that began from the moment Mrs Singh reached out to me. My limbs felt numb, but my thoughts raced as I walked to the car park. I sensed an ordeal ahead and I could not shake the growing feeling of apprehension that sometimes gripped me when I entered the courtroom for a difficult trial.

Photo – Take 3

The day Mother Superior rushed into the refectory excited, out of breath, saying that our prayers had been answered, I felt relief because the convent would not have to close, our community would not have to disperse to houses in distant locations and I could remain here to complete preparation for final vows. Sister Margaret, the Mother Superior, said that someone had come to our rescue by offering to make a donation. She promised to have more news for us by suppertime when she expected to receive more details. My concern was to avoid any disruptions that would hinder my taking final vows. The convent had given me a home and I had made up my mind to spend the rest of my life there. It had offered an ocean of peace after the rough, uncertain life in the shelter. I remember the joy I felt when Sister Margaret said that I could live in the convent on condition that I consider joining the order when I was old enough to make a decision about my future. I told her there and then that I would join the order, but she said I was too young to decide and I would have to wait till I was older. Knowing that I wouldn't have to live in the shelter any more calmed the anxiety that had gnawed at my gut. I knew I would miss Alicia and Ariel, but they were older than me and were going to classes every day at the training centre across town. Sister said they could come to visit me at the convent, and in the beginning they came often. Many years have gone by and they're now busy with their careers.

There was a tremor of excitement in the house as we waited for more news from Sister Margaret. Today, I was given duties in the garden and I'd spent the time pulling up weeds, collecting young plants for cultivation in the nursery and cutting blooms for the vases in the chapel. After supper, Mother Superior stood up and announced that the donor would be selling a work of art and he would donate the funds to the convent. She said the donor had offered to bring the piece to show us on Sunday.

It is late afternoon on Sunday and we're sitting in the refectory waiting for the donor. The door opens and Mother Superior ushers in a man who is carrying a large frame covered with a grey cloth. He is short and stocky and the frame is almost as tall as he is. He seems to struggle slightly under the weight of it. Something about him is familiar. Perhaps it's his gait. He walks with a slight limp. His back is turned to us as he follows Sister to the head table at the front of the room. She helps him prop the frame against the stone column near one end of the table and she motions for him to sit. His cheeks are sunken and he has a mop of shaggy grey hair woven into locks that tumble in a tangle to his shoulders. One of his ears is missing a piece as though a chunk was bitten from it. His eyes are set deep in bony sockets and they are piercing as his gaze sweeps over us. He is older, but I recognize the steel set to his jaw and the lips drawn together in a thin line. I would recognize him if he were skeletal with the skin drawn tight over his skull. I shift so that I'm sitting behind the sister on the bench at the table in front of ours, out of his line of vision. I bow my head as Mother Superior introduces him.

"Sisters, this is Mr Zodi Alias who has offered to make a generous donation to the convent. He has brought a photograph from his collection which, he says, he will sell to get some of the funds he plans to give to us. He thought we might want to see the work that will be contributing to the gift he will give. I thank him on our behalf." She turns to him. "Will you say a few words to the sisters, Mr Alias?"

He stands. There is a slight stoop to his shoulders. He thrusts his hands deep into the pockets of his jacket. His attempt at a smile is a grimace.

"Thank you, Mother Superior, for allowing me to make a small contribution to the convent. I was invited to make a presentation at the town council meeting last month when the mayor spoke about the difficulties the convent has been experiencing. The convent has been a part of this community for as long as I can remember. I attended the prep school that used to be run by the sisters. I and everyone in the community regret that the school had to be closed. The council wants the convent to remain in this community and I'm sure you'll be happy to know that they will be organizing fundraisers to make sure this happens. I want to contribute by donating the funds from selling this photograph. We all hope that the donations will usher in a period of growth so that the convent can thrive again." He pauses and turns to look at Sister Margaret. "Would you like to unveil it, Sister, or shall I?"

Sister Margaret motions with her hand that he should go ahead. He places his hand on the frame, pauses, and turns to us.

"This is a work in a series I did a long time ago. The entire series, except for this one, was bought by a gallery in London and it has brought me much recognition and good fortune. It was hard to part with this one. I kept it for good luck. Sister, I hope you all do not mind the subject matter."

He clutches a fold of the cloth and in one sweeping motion pulls it off the frame. I gasp and Mother Superior looks at me. Within the gilt-edged frame is an enlarged photograph of three females in a huddle at the centre. They're all nude and two are shown in profile, facing each other, their heads tilted towards the third who is facing the camera. The breasts of the two in profile are visible but their bodies hide most of the third who is shorter than they are. Her head is bent forward towards theirs so one does not see her full face. I recognize them right away. The one facing is me, the one on the left is Alicia and the other one is Ariel. My heartbeat quickens. I feel the blood rush to my face and my head feels light.

"Isn't it lovely?" I hear Mr Alias through a thick fog that has invaded my ears. "It is a gelatin silver photo. I shot and developed it myself. Notice the tonal range of the bodies, the deep, dark of this girl . . .," he says as he points to Ariel, ". . . and the variation to grey tones in the complexion of the other two."

He moves his hand in a caress over the figures. "The contrast is superbly captured, even if I say so myself. Notice how the arrangement within

the composition highlights the clean lines of their bodies. It's lovely . . .
a classic." He takes a deep breath, pauses and looks around the room.

I bow my head lower and wonder whether he might have seen and
recognized me even with the veil covering my hair and a bit of my forehead
and cheeks. My anxiety increases as I wonder whether Mother Superior
and the other sisters might recognize me. A younger me, for sure, but my
face hasn't changed all that much in fifteen years. Mr Alias continues.

"I expect it to fetch a very good price. The quality and composition are
excellent. The mayor has suggested that we have a formal ceremony to
present the photo to the buyer and to give you the donation, Sister. He
thinks this will attract a positive response and more donations. He also
suggested that we could invite the models in the photo to the handing-
over ceremony, if we can locate them. What do you think?"

"We will leave these details to you and the members of the council,
Mr Alias." Sister picks up the cloth and drapes it over the photograph.
"We are grateful for the contribution you have promised. Sisters, let's
give a round of applause to Mr Alias." He picks up the photograph and
she ushers him out of the room as we applaud to show our appreciation.

It is now almost time for vespers and I make a beeline for the chapel.
My head is spinning as I walk along. I do not want to be identified as one
of the models in the photo and I'm sure neither Alicia nor Ariel will want
this. I need to let them know so we can figure out how to avoid the public
exhibition and gossip this is sure to bring. It may not be an issue for them,
but it is for me, especially if Mother Superior suspects something. She
glanced at me curiously when she led Mr Alias out of the room.

Alicia

I was in the middle of a shoot this morning when Anna called to tell me
that Mr Alias had visited the convent and was going to donate money
towards its renovation. She was afraid that he had recognized her. It's been
years now since he took that photo she described. We were young then.
Anna is the youngest. We've moved on and I don't think the revelation
that I'm one of the girls in the photo would matter or harm my career

in any way. Come to think of it, I may just get a boost out of it. Anna said he described the photograph in superlative terms. She identified us immediately and worried that Sister Margaret might have made her out too. I don't suppose the publicity would matter to Ariel either. She's a successful lawyer. Anna said she would call her, but I'll get in touch with her anyway. She was always protective of Anna. I still think of Ariel as Flame of the Triple A Team which is what we called ourselves. I used to call her Flame when she would stand up for Anna. I remember the time when she leaped on Mr Alias's back and bit off a piece of his ear because Anna was in tears when he brought her back to the shelter after a solo session. He howled and shrugged her off and she spat the bloody piece of flesh right in his face.

Ariel was impulsive. She acted first and asked questions later – if at all. That day, she took one look at Anna crying, her eyes red, her clothes rumpled and Mr A clutching her arm with one hand and holding a small box of chocolates in the other. The box fell from his hand when Ariel leaped on his back. The rest of us in the room ran to pick them up and we ate them. Anna didn't like chocolates, but she always came back from sessions with chocolates she said Mr A had given her. Ariel didn't eat any either, but some of the children in the shelter made friends with Anna just to get chocolates from her. She always offered them to me first because she knew I liked them.

That shelter wasn't much of a place to stay but they brought us there after the storm and the landslides. We were lucky the trucks came to take us away before the mud came down the hillside. I wish they had come earlier so our father and mother would have been safe too. Things would have been different if they were in the shelter with us to take care of us. They would not have let Mr A take us off for photos. There was no one in charge, it seemed. We were lucky when the Sisters of Sorrowful Passion took over responsibility for the shelter. After they came at least they didn't allow Mr Alias to take any of us for photo sessions and we didn't see him again. Anna made up her mind from back then to join the convent. I really don't care if they know we are the models and invite us to the ceremony. It may be bad for Anna, but it would be good for my career.

Ariel

It's strange how life goes in cycles. Who would have thought that Zodi Alias would resurface in our lives after all these years? He should have stayed wherever it is he went after the sisters took over the running of the shelter. Anna didn't tell me much but I knew he had hurt her when she came back with bruises on her arms. She kept blaming herself and saying it was her fault. I couldn't understand that. She was barely ten then. She always gave in to Alicia and me, playing the games we wanted, giving us her sweets. As for the chocolates she said Mr Alias had given her, I didn't want any of them. I couldn't understand why she was always crying when he brought her back and why she was the only one he would give chocolates. I've figured it out since then. They were a bribe to keep her from saying what he did to her. I'm sure he did more than box her around. He must have hit her for a reason but she never told me. When I asked her, all she did was cry and say it was her fault.

I saw red the last time she came back in tears with those marks on her arms. I would have bitten off more than a piece of his ear if I could have. I told him I would tell what he had done, but back then I wouldn't have known what to tell. Soon after that the sisters took over care for the orphans and he never came back to the shelter. When Alicia told Sister what I had done she said I had an unbridled temper and I needed to tame it, but she didn't punish me for biting his ear. I've figured out now what happened with Anna, but didn't then. Neither did Alicia. Even now, I don't think she has a clue about what went on. All she cares about now is her modelling career. Mr Alias is something else. I never trusted him, peering at us with narrowed eyes as though trying to see right into our souls. Perhaps that's why he's considered to be a celebrated photographer. Perhaps he was trying to capture our innocence and hoping to transfer some of it to himself. Or perhaps he's just an evil person. An accent on the *o* in his name would describe exactly what he is. Rubbish. That's what he is – rubbish! What a name! – Designated Rubbish! Good thing he left and never came back. Anna is safe now and happy. Nothing must change that.

I don't see the need for us to be present at any donation ceremony. He must not come back into our lives. Alicia doesn't mind publicity but I don't need it and he must stay away from Anna. I'll send a letter to the mayor to indicate that the models are my clients and they do not wish to be contacted for any purposes related to the photograph and ceremony. That should do it.

Anna

I'm relieved. Ariel called to tell me what she plans to do. There's no chance that we'll be identified and asked to appear at a ceremony that celebrates our nakedness. What would it look like, me standing there in my novice habit next to a photograph of me in the nude? I can imagine tongues wagging and making up stories. Mother Superior would definitely not be comfortable with that either. It isn't as if we offered ourselves as models to Mr Alias. He took advantage of us when supervision was lax. With everyone focused on recovery from the disaster, he pretty much had the liberty to use us for his own ends. Over the years I've shut out memories about our early days in the shelter and most of it has been a blank; at least it was until Sister Margaret and Mr A walked in with that photo. Just the sight of him made my stomach churn and every night now I have nightmares. Something from those days flashes in my mind and I wake up in a sweat, my chest hurting as it did then.

That Sunday he showed up with Sister I spent a long time after vespers praying in the chapel and in my cell. As soon as I lay down and closed my eyes images flashed through my mind. I was sitting on the floor, crying, and Mr A was holding my arm, shaking me and telling me I was a snivelling idiot. I was hurting all over and believed I had done something wrong. I remembered how he changed suddenly, gave me a box of chocolates, stroked my hair, hugged me and asked me to stop crying, like my father used to do when I was small, except that it was different and I didn't want Mr A to touch me. I closed my eyes tight and prayed hard so I wouldn't remember more. Now the old, afraid feelings have come back with the memories. I think I should talk to Mother Superior about this, but I know she will just say I should go to confession. She believes that going to confession is a panacea for every ill.

This morning I did a good job of trimming the rose bushes. The blooms are gorgeous and I'll put them in the vases around the altar and at the base of the crucifix at the side. The chapel always looks bright and cheerful when I put in fresh flowers. I think Mother Superior will be pleased although she sometimes tells me not to overdo things. Not enough flowers and she complains. Full vases and she shakes her head. I don't know what to think. How can one overdo things by praising God with an abundance of flowers? It will soon be midday. I'll stay here until the bell rings for the Angelus, "The Angel of the Lord declared unto Mary . . ." How pure in soul one must be to have an angel visit. If it was my fault, how burdened my soul must be. I can't recall if I ever confessed anything in those days. I didn't remember any details until the nightmares started. How much I would give for the peace of forgetfulness.

The bell rings three times for the start of the Angelus. I join the recitation with the sisters who come into the chapel. Today I've decided to skip lunch as a penance and I kneel before the altar for the entire hour and pray. I hear footsteps come into the chapel and realize I must have dozed off while reciting the chaplet of Divine Mercy. I try to begin again where I think I left off. I run my fingers over my rosary beads. The steps continue all the way up to the altar where I'm kneeling. I close my eyes and try to concentrate on the recitation. Someone kneels on the step next to me. I keep my eyes closed and clutch each bead deliberately as I pray. I hear the breath wheezing from the person next to me. I hear the voice and my eyes open wide.

"So this is where you've been hiding." I glance sideways and see Mr Alias staring at me. I move quickly to stand but he puts his hand firmly on my shoulder.

"Don't get up. I've only come because I thought I recognized you when I was here last time and I've come to see if I was right. You haven't changed much, just grown more beautiful as I knew you would."

I brush his hand away and I stand up to face him. "How did you get in here? You're not supposed to be here."

"I was at the gate looking into the garden. I saw when you came in here. I waited for a while and slipped in when the sisters came out."

"You shouldn't be here and if you don't leave I'll call Mother Superior."

"Got a little feisty, haven't you? I want to apologize for what happened before. First, that's what I came to do, and second, I want to make amends and offer you an opportunity to . . ."

"I don't need or want anything that you may have to offer. I am where I want and need to be."

"I would like to make up . . . I can offer you a life of comfort and ease, if you agreed . . ."

"I don't want anything from you. Please leave now."

"You don't understand. You've been on my mind and I'd like a chance to make up for . . ."

"You've done enough. You took advantage of me."

"No, it wasn't that at all. Don't you remember? You missed your family. You were crying for your father and I . . ."

"I was a child and you took advantage of me. You shouldn't be here. Go away."

"You're not letting me finish what I'm saying. Interrupting like you used to. That's irritating, and as I used to tell you before, you need to stop it."

He grabs my arm and steps closer to me. I pull away and hear a tearing sound as he clutches my sleeve which rips down to my wrist. I move backwards to stand next to the crucifix. I knock over one of the vases with roses I had placed on the table next to it. The copper vase clangs as it falls on the stone step.

"Leave now or I'll scream . . . I'll tell Sister about you. I'll tell her what you did . . ."

"You little liar. You're still a snivelling little liar. I did nothing to you. Being here hasn't done you one ounce of good. You think covering your head with a veil and your body with this habit can change what you are?"

He moves closer to where I'm standing, reaches forward and pulls the veil off my head. I hold on to the edge of the table next to the crucifix.

"Leave, Mr Alias."

"The least you could do is thank me for offering you the chance of a good life. You would be an excellent model for my photos" – he laughs out loud and continues – "even in this frumpy habit. Think it over. You might change your mind."

"Get out and leave me alone. This is a chapel! Go away."

"Why? Didn't I give you chocolates? I could give you much more now."

"As far as I'm concerned you're . . . Go away!"

He draws his lips into a thin line and his eyes narrow to a slit as he takes another step towards me. I step back, clutch the crucifix and pick it up. It's heavier than I thought it was, but I lift it with both hands above my shoulder.

"So you've learned how to fight, have you?" He laughs and takes another step towards me. I swing the crucifix with all my strength and it slams into his forearm which he raises to protect his face. He steps into the puddle of water from the copper vase, slips, clutches at my habit and it tears away in his grasp as he falls. I hear his head hit the stone with a loud clunk. There's a fog in my ears and everything is a blur. I drop the crucifix, clutch at the fragment of cloth on my shoulder and run towards the main door.

Someone is standing there. It's Mother Superior. She grabs the felt cloth off the table next to the door. The bulletins fly in every direction. She begins to open the cloth as she turns towards me. I lift my hand to hide my face, rush past her and run virtually naked into the sunlit garden.

Torn Pages

Dawn slowly turned the pages of the unlined leather journal. There were two sheets torn away from the spine. She had found it in his drawer when she was tidying up after her mother's death. She hadn't bothered to look through it until now that she was clearing the house of their belongings. This was obviously a journal he had kept to record information about his family and important events in his life. The first few pages were about his ancestors, his great-grandfather and great-grandmother who were born in Barbados. His grandfather and grandmother who had migrated to Trinidad where he worked as a contractor before moving to Saint Lucia. The entries were sketchy. He had only jotted down important information: names, dates of birth and baptism, schools attended, names and spouses of his siblings, dates of marriages and deaths. There were some blank spaces where he seemed not to have the information or forgot to enter it. But those were few.

The more detailed information began with his own page on which he listed all the schools he had attended, the examinations he had taken, the list of jobs he had had, starting from the age of seventeen when he had graduated from secondary school. He had listed all the training he had received in relation to the various jobs, the places he had gone to be trained and the starting and ending dates of training. At the bottom of his page he had two question marks, each one on a different line. Continuing on a fresh page overleaf he had entered the date of his marriage, the name of his spouse, Lenore, and the dates of birth and baptism of their two children, Dawn and Garnet. On the same page he had included information about his wife's parents, the schools she attended, the dates of her baptism, first communion, confirmation, school examinations and school leaving. He put the names of Dawn and Garnet on separate pages and had begun a similar list for each one. His last entry on Dawn's page was a note that she had won the island scholarship and had gone off to study medicine.

When she first discovered the journal she had fetched a pen and completed his own page with the date and time of his death, and the date of his funeral. She concluded her mother's page in the same way. Her mother had died two years after her father. She kept the book with her and entered details about herself and Garnet. She wondered about the two torn pages, one which had been ripped from the space between the entries he had made for her and Garnet, and the other after Garnet's entries. She held up Garnet's page to the light looking for indentations that might have remained from his writing on the previous page. There was nothing she could detect and the writing about Garnet covered the entire page. She recalled an incident that had occurred one year when she had returned home on holiday and it occurred to her that it had everything to do with one of the pages.

The first torn page –

He sat hunched over his desk, shirtsleeves rolled halfway up his forearm. He was checking off items in a large ledger on his desk and setting aside receipts as he went systematically through the pile on the desk. Several of them were missing and he would have to go into the filing room to search for them. It was hot and he preferred not to move away from the main office where the ceiling fans sent out warm currents of air that stirred up the dust he could see in the shaft of sunlight that pierced through the window into the room.

The day hadn't started right. The baby had been irritable all night and he and Lenore had taken turns waking up to soothe and rock her back to sleep. He had got up late with a headache and had had to trot almost the whole way to get to work on time. He wasn't looking forward to a repeat of the night before.

"Sir, you can tell me where the paymaster is?" She must have been standing there for a while but he hadn't noticed.

"I'm the paymaster. How can I help you?"

"Mr Niles say we must pick up our pay from main office today, so I come for that and somebody send me in here to speak to the paymaster."

"Well, you're in the right place but you'll have to wait a moment because everything is already locked in the vault as it's the end of the day. Have a seat and I'll be right back." He put the receipts into a drawer and cleared a space on the desk before going into the file room at the back of the office where the vault was located. He got as far as the door and turned back.

"I forgot to ask your name. I need to know to get your envelope."

"Millicent, Millicent St Ange."

He wrote it down on a slip of paper and returned to the file room. St Ange was a common Saint Lucian name. He wondered whether she was related to his friend Morris. He returned to the desk with a ledger and an envelope.

"Here you are. I need you to sign right here." He put the ledger in front of her and placed his index finger on the spot where she should sign. Her skirt had inched up above her knees as she sat down and crossed one leg over the other. He noticed that her legs were shapely and her thighs were firm and smooth.

"Which St Ange family do you belong to? Are you related to Morris?" he asked.

"No, I don't know any Morris."

"Okay, which family . . .?"

"We are from down south," she said quickly, "but I live up here during the week because of the job."

"I see."

She put the pen down and he handed her the envelope with her pay. She said "good afternoon" as she rose to leave and he picked up the ledger and watched as she walked to the door.

"Please close the door behind you," he called out. "It's closing time and I'm about to leave."

He locked the vault and the storeroom, turned off the lights and the fan and put on his jacket. Everyone had already left and he had to make sure the place was locked up. It was raining when he went outside. Several people were huddled under the veranda sheltering from the downpour. He saw her standing alone, off to one side of the sidewalk. He inched his way slowly over to where she stood.

"That's a steady downpour, isn't it?"

"Yes, the rain not stopping at all."

"Looks like we'll be stuck here for a while, don't you think? How will you get home?"

"Oh, I have my umbrella right here in my bag. Once the rain ease up a little, I will go home."

"So where is home?"

"On Peynier Street."

"Oh, I pass there every day on my way to and from work."

"Look, it lighten up a little. If you want a shelter you can walk with me up to Peynier Street."

The rain was slanting down as they set off. He walked a little away from her so as not to use up too much space under the umbrella. His left arm and shoulder were exposed and absorbing the drizzle and the drip from the umbrella.

By the time they got to Peynier Street it was raining heavily and she was struggling to hold the umbrella upright against a strong gust that tunnelled through the row of houses lining both sides of the street. She stopped in front of a modest house. The brown paint was faded and peeling off the wood in some parts.

"I living here," she said. "If you want you can come in and shelter till the rain stop."

Next door there was a two-storey house with a wide veranda above the first floor that extended across the sidewalk. It was held up by four sturdy iron poles at the front.

"I'll shelter under that veranda," he said. "It's dry there close to the front door of the house, so I'll stand there. Thanks for the umbrella." He sprinted across the short space that separated the two houses and stood in the dry part of the veranda, his back leaning against the woodwork close to the front door. He could see her standing still in the rain for a while, then she opened the door and went in. A light mist drifted under the veranda, spreading a damp film over the entire space. He drew upright, pressed his back against the house and buttoned his jacket.

It was getting dark and the street lights came on, casting a faint glow on the small pools that had collected around the poles. He saw the light of her front room go on and the window shutters pulled open and shut again. The street was suddenly illumined by a bright flash of lightning and a moment later the sky seemed to crack open with a peal of thunder that rattled the front door and the shutters of the house where he stood. He did not see her front door open but he felt an insistent tugging on his arm and she was there, face pale with terror and holding on tightly to his arm. She had run out without the umbrella because her hair was dripping wet and strands were plastered across her cheeks.

"Mr Paymaster, why you don't come inside and shelter? Look how here getting wet and the thunder start up. I fraid the thunder." Another peal drowned out her voice and she squeezed his arm more tightly.

He was about to reply to reassure her that the storm would soon pass when another flash of lightning brightened the street. As the thunder started, she tugged at his arm and seemingly without volition his body followed the figure that pulled him through the rain and her front door into a dimly lit room. She slammed the door shut just as another thunderous crack splintered the air Now she was clutching him with both arms, her body pressed tightly against his.

The rain had ceased when he left two hours later. As he walked through the wet, potholed street on his way home, he tried to reconstruct the events of the last two hours without much success; but the lassitude that invaded his body informed him well enough and now he worried about what he would say to Lenore about his whereabouts during the storm.

Over the next few weeks he took a long route to and from work just to avoid Peynier Street. Then one afternoon, as he was tidying his desk and packing to close up, the door opened. She walked in and without asking sat down in the chair facing him. He masked his surprise and said too quickly,

"How are you? How can I help you?"

"Now you aksing me. Weeks gone by and you ain't stop by once to aks how I doing. I have to come here for you to aks me. Ay, ay, what is dat, eh?"

He used the most professional tone he could muster.

"What happened the night of the storm was a mistake. I had no intention of coming into your house. What happened was a big mistake."

"Now you saying it was a mistake. That's not what I hear you saying then. I hear you saying 'joy, joy'. Dat don't mean the same thing as mistake and is 'joy, what joy" I hear you say loud like the thunder itself."

"Sometimes things happen that shouldn't and this was one of them. Tell me how I can help you so you can . . ."

"How you going help me? How? The joy dat inside me now going to need a father. Tell me how you going help me wid dat."

His knuckles whitened with the tension of his grip and the ruler he was holding with both hands broke.

"That's impossible. That was just . . ."

"One sweet moment, Mr Paymaster," she finished the sentence. "And look, I don't even know your name. Not even dat you tell me. But is a little paymaster in there for sure."

"Listen, I'm married. This won't work out. If you need some money . . . but just that one time . . . How can I be sure it's mine?"

"Haiiii!" She let out a loud long shriek, half a laugh, half a cry. He looked around quickly to see if there was anyone else in the office. There wasn't. He looked at her as she stood up, held on to the edge of the desk and leaned towards him. "So is what you saying? What you saying? You think I? . . . Ha!" Another loud exclamation and she looked down shaking her head from side to side. She looked at him, her eyes narrowed to slits. "I don't want nothing from you, you hear? Nothing. And I don't want to have nothing to do with you again, you hear me? Nothing. You can tek duh joy you say you had and shove it up your paymaster behind, you hear me?" She spun on her heels and was out of the door before he could even blink.

He sat stunned for a while, then he rushed to the door, opened it, looked left then right, but there was no one on the sidewalk. He went back into the office and slumped forward at the edge of his chair, his elbows on the desk. What a mess, he thought. How was he going to get out of it? What if she went to Lenore? A cold sweat seeped out of his pores and he felt nauseous. He ran to the toilet and emptied his stomach of everything he'd eaten for lunch. It was well past closing time so he finished clearing his desk and left. He crawled into bed as soon as he got home. Lenore made him ginger tea and he took one sip and set the cup aside. He fell into a troubled sleep and when she finally got to bed after getting the baby to sleep, he was sleeping fitfully and muttering incoherently. She thought she heard him say "it was a mistake" but she was tired and fell asleep without trying to figure what could be the matter with him. The next day he woke up more like his usual self and blamed his indisposition on something he had bought and eaten on the way to the office.

He lived a nightmare for the next two weeks, working very late because he feared that one day he would go home to find that she had told Lenore about the affair. Of all the things he dreaded it was that Lenore would leave him. He loved her, loved their child and the tidy family life they had built together. The thought of any disruption to that haven which he credited himself with having created filled him with dread.

After the first two weeks had passed with no word from her or an appearance at his office, he began to feel relieved. He still avoided the street on which she lived. He knew where her house was and what the front room looked like but he didn't know much else about her except that her name was Millicent St Ange and she had done work for the company he worked for. He berated himself almost daily for having been an idiot to accept her offer of shelter, but sometimes while he was doing that he would recall the moments in her front room when their bodies were interlocked on her sofa with the thunder crashing about their ears as one of the most intense moments of passion he had experienced. "Unbridled passion – nothing but that," he sometimes muttered to himself. Then the guilt would surface, then the discomfort, and his stomach would contract and he would be miserable.

When nothing happened by the end of the third week, he thought she had given up and he felt relieved. He promised himself never to let such a situation happen again. Then his conscience started to get the better of him and he thought that if he had indeed fathered a child the least he could do would be to offer her some financial support. It would be tough because he made precious little and he knew Lenore would ask questions about the reduced pay, but he thought he could make up a convincing story perhaps about insurance or an investment in a sou-sou, a group savings and pay-out scheme, or something like that. He remembered that Lenore didn't believe in sou-sous so he would have to steer clear of that but she might buy into the insurance policy story. After another month had gone by, the thought about his responsibility was more persistent and he found himself taking routes that brought him closer to Peynier Street but he still hadn't summoned the courage to go there.

He told himself that he needed to be careful because Lenore had noticed that he was distracted and she was asking a lot of questions about his work and what he was doing. Sometimes she was so persistent that he thought she must have heard something. It was a small community and if Millicent had told anyone about her plight the news would inevitably get to Lenore. When she questioned him he would become anxious and suspicious. He would give evasive answers and that would only prompt her to ask him more questions. Twice he had shouted in exasperation and left the room and she hadn't spoken to him for days. He had made up by buying her mints and chocolates, the ones she liked from the drugstore on Main Street, and taking her to a movie on the weekend.

They walked through the streets holding hands and there was only one moment of discomfort when she wanted to know why he chose to take a longer route when they could have walked along Peynier Street to get to the cinema faster. He made up a story about wanting to spend a longer time walking with her as they used to do when they were courting. She accepted that and held on to his hand more tightly. He told himself what he had said was true and he would try to have these outings more often.

One day after work he summoned the courage to go to Millicent's house to say that he would support the child by giving her a monthly allowance but he would tell her that he didn't want her telling people the child was his. So he walked to Peynier Street, stopped in front of her house, looked around to make sure no one who knew him was around, then he knocked on the door. The shutters were up and fastened so he could not tell if there was any light inside. After a few moments he knocked more loudly but no one came to open the door. He went away thinking that she may have gone to her family in the country, but every week, once or twice, he would stop by the house on Peynier Street and knock on the door. He thought he needed to redeem himself by making this gesture of an offer of financial help. He told himself it was for that reason he would persist until he could make an arrangement. But every time he stopped at the house and got no response, he felt more relieved at the thought that she had left. After following that routine at least every week for two months he decided to stop, convincing himself that he had tried to do the right thing. He settled into an easy frame of mind, became less tense, and life resumed its even tenor of the night before the storm.

One sultry afternoon as he sat in his office going through the list of workers to prepare the payroll, the mailman walked in and handed him a slip for a registered letter. He signed the form and walked over to the post office to collect the letter. It was a brown envelope with a postmark from England but the handwriting was unfamiliar. He waited until he got back to his desk to open the envelope. He pulled out a single blue sheet of paper on which was a letter of one paragraph. He read:

> *Dear Mr Paymaster, I writing to tell you that you don't have to worry about nothing to do with me. I gone and I not coming back. I just letting you know that the little paymaster born and I give him your family name as his first name. He is Charlemagne Joy St Ange so you will know him when you meet him. I not coming back but who knows one day he will not want to come and look for his father? I just letting you know Mr Paymaster, Hilaire Charlemagne. Bon jou.*

She ended the letter with the French Creole greeting meaning "good day", but she didn't sign her name. There was no return address on either the envelope or the letter. He knew there was a small link to him on the other side of the Atlantic but he was unconnected. She had done her research and had found out his name and other things. He was sure she was well informed.

When he got home that evening he entered a note on a fresh page of his journal. Charlemagne St Ange, Illegitimate son. Mother: Millicent St Ange. Exact date of birth – not known – Year 1944. He fastened that page with a paper clip to the blank page following the one on which he had made entries for his daughter Dawn. He put the book under a pile of papers in the only drawer of his desk at home and locked the drawer.

They were sitting in the living room after dinner and she was regaling them with stories about the cadavers she had had to open up to study and analyse.

"If I never see the insides of another human being, I'll be happy."

"Then you chose the wrong profession, my dear," Hilaire said. "And now you're thinking you would like to specialize in surgery after you graduate. So, you're doomed to a life of viewing human entrails, I'm afraid."

"Yeah, I guess so. One gets used to it anyway, and I actually like the idea of opening up a body to repair it."

"Those stories you told us were really yucky, Dawn," Garnet piped up. "That one about how the rice and peas spilled out of his stomach when you opened it was the worst."

"Yeah. He didn't even have time to digest it. His heart gave out."

"Guess what, sis. Your stories must have inspired me because I've decided to apply for medicine at Mona. If I get in, I'll be there with you next year."

"Hey, Garn, that's great. Why didn't you tell me before?"

The phone rang and they looked at each other.

"Well, aren't you going to answer?" Lenore prodded. I suppose you're waiting for me or your father to get up. Garnet, please answer the phone."

They heard his voice somewhat muffled from the next room, then he came back and said, "Dad, a man on the phone; says his name is

Charlemagne St Ange. He said he's visiting the island and wants to come and see you."

There was a pregnant silence, then Hilaire cleared his throat, puffed on his cigarette, coughed, got up and said, "I'll take the call."

"Oh, he hung up, Dad. He said he's just down the road and he can be here in a few minutes. He just wanted to know if you were home. When I told him you're here he said he'll come along."

Hilaire froze. The cigarette hung loosely from lips that seemed lifeless.

"Are you okay?" Lenore asked.

He sat back heavily in his seat and drew long and hard on his cigarette. Then he spoke, puffs of smoke coming out with words which he seemed to have trouble putting together into a coherent sentence. "This is, I mean, I meant to tell you . . . Maybe you remember a long time ago . . . how do I say this? Lenore, this is going to be . . . perhaps we should go inside so I can tell you . . ."

Just then, a car drew up in the driveway. A door slammed and someone ran up the stairs leading to the front door which was open as it usually was when they sat in the living room. A young man, about Dawn's age stood in the doorway.

"Hello," he said. "I'm Charlemagne, Charlemagne St Ange. My mother says you're my father." He had a distinctive British accent and he was smiling as though expecting familiarity. Hilaire seemed to have frozen in his seat. Lenore stood up and went forward to shake his hand.

"Come in," she said. "Have a seat."

Hilaire stood up at that point to shake his hand. Dawn could see immediately the resemblance between her father and the young man who leaned forward eagerly towards Hilaire as though expecting him to embrace him.

"Have a seat, have a seat," Hilaire said quickly, gesturing towards a chair.

It was Lenore who offered him a drink and asked him innumerable questions about himself and his mother, about his life in England. He chatted cheerfully, answering her questions and elaborating as well. He said his mother had lived in England for several years. She was working as a nurse and was married to a man from Barbados. He had been born in England and he had one sibling, a brother who was two years younger than he was. He said he would be leaving the island on the following day. He had been to the south to visit his mother's family, but he had promised his mother that he would visit his father and meet the rest of his family. Garnet seemed pleased to discover he had a brother and they exchanged addresses and phone numbers before Charlemagne left.

"Fancy," he said, "your first name is the same as our family name; but Joy? I always thought of that as a girl's name. Fancy your mom calling you Joy."

"That," Lenore said, "is no accident, I'm sure."

Dawn sat quietly taking in everything and feeling badly for her mother, who, she knew, was putting on a brave front. When he finally left, Lenore shut the front door, turned, swished her skirt as she did when she was annoyed or flustered, exclaimed, "Well!", then walked, head high, her back straight and stiff, down the corridor and into her bedroom. Hilaire was still sitting in his chair puffing on cigarettes when Dawn and Garnet went in to bed.

She ran her finger over the edge of the torn page. She remembered that incident clearly. She guessed that one torn page must have had the name Charlemagne Joy St Ange written on it. She picked up her pen, turned to a clean page and started writing his name and putting in the few details she had. She would get some more from Garnet and would probably follow up herself by getting in touch with Charlemagne. She had not seen him again since the night he had visited and a few years had elapsed. He must not have known about Hilaire's death because he never wrote; at least Lenore didn't mention it and he wasn't at the funeral. She had no particular feelings for him. He was a stranger who had come into their life for a fleeting moment. She had felt some resentment at the time because she knew her mother had been hurt. Now she was indifferent. But she knew he existed and she should get in touch with him to let him know about their father.

The second torn page –

The phone rang. Dawn had just walked into the room. She had had a long day at the hospital where she was doing a residency in Surgery.

"Hello."

"May I speak with Dawn Charlemagne?"

"This is she."

"I'm returning your call. I'm Hilaire Charlemagne and I got a message that you wanted to speak with me."

"Oh yes, I called. I saw your photograph in Sunday's paper; you know, the social section with the article and photos about the reception following the launch of your company. I thought it curious that your name is exactly the same as my father's and, if I may say so, I detected a slight family resemblance. I hope you don't think me inquisitive, but I thought I'd call to follow up with you just in case."

There was a brief silence, then he said, "Well, my mother never spoke much about my father except to say that he was from one of the islands. Before she died she said she didn't know if he was alive or dead but while I was growing up she sometimes said that as far as she was concerned he was dead."

"That's interesting because my father was from one of the islands too, but he's dead now. It's curious that you would have his exact name and it isn't a common name, wouldn't you agree?"

"Yes, I guess so. I wouldn't mind at all to discover I have family somewhere. I have no siblings that I know of. My mother can't help now, but I've got a box of hers with a diary and some papers. Why not meet for lunch? I will bring the diary because that's the only thing in the box that might give some clues. The papers all have to do with personal business matters."

They met and he brought a leather book with lined pages. There was writing on most of them and some blank pages at the back. There was a pocket along the length of the back cover but it seemed empty. She said, "Perhaps the entries will tell us something."

"To be honest, I haven't got around to reading it. I meant to do that but felt that I would be intruding into her very personal affairs. I can let you have it to check but you must give it back."

"Of course I will. I can check the entries to see if she met my father when he was in Barbados for some training. I'll let you know what I find out."

That evening she started to read the diary. There were sections where Madge, Hilaire's mother, had made entries for several consecutive days and there were parts where she had made just one entry for an entire month. The first set of entries that seemed relevant were in early 1946. The first one was dated Monday 14th January. She read:

> Training started today. The instructor had us all introduce ourselves. Most of the people in the group seem older but there are six or eight about my age. One of the men caught my attention. The girl next to me distracted me just as he began to introduce himself so I didn't catch his name. Heard him say he has a family and he works with the government. Must follow up.

The next entry was four days later on the 18th. Dawn read:

> Interesting group. We're getting to know each other and the sessions can be heated – much discussion. Found out his name is Hilaire Charlemagne. Checked the list and he's from St Lucia. A good-looking hunk but he keeps to himself mostly. Seems nice. Not sure I like getting homework assignments every day – as if we have nothing else to do. I guess six weeks of this won't hurt. Have an idea we can start a liming group; would be relaxing after a week of work. Will check the others.

On the 26th she had scribbled the following:

> Had a blast last night. Six of us agreed to a lime after class. We went to Mike's Café on Broad Street for a drink and it was fun. We stayed there for hours. Ate fish cutters and drank rum and Coke. Think I had one too many because I laughed a lot. Think we all had too much to drink. Sat beside Mr Charlemagne. Said his name is Hilaire and we didn't need to stand on ceremony – so we're on first name basis. He has a great sense of humour; he gave so many jokes we couldn't stop laughing. Hilaire the Hilarious I called him. He laughed. Great lime!

There was an entry for 2nd February which read,

> *Another great lime. Must watch how much I drink. Was a bit off balance when I stood up to leave and Hilaire offered to walk me home. Quite the gentleman he is; very proper. He wouldn't come in although I invited him to. Said he was a bit tipsy himself. We agreed to have an end of training party after the last class. I offered to have it at my home. Everyone agreed to bring something. Should be a good fete but we still have a couple weeks for limes at Mike's.*

On the 23rd of February there was a long entry. She read:

> *Having an end of training party was the best idea I've had in a long time. We had a blast last night. It was wild . . . Between them the men brought three demijohns of Mount Gay rum – could have had two parties with that. I'll have a supply of rum for the rest of the year. Haven't danced so much in a long time. Hilaire is such a dancer! He really loosened up last night. Oh what a few rums can do! He was in the middle of the floor showing off his moves. And what moves! Guess he was tight but it was hard to tell. Guess he holds his liquor well. We were really into it by the end of the party. When the others were leaving he said he was staying to have one last dance. What a dance! Guess we were both hot! This morning he could hardly bring himself to look at me. I made a great omelette with saltfish and onion filling but he said he wasn't hungry. He gave the cutest apology – said he was drunk and was sorry if he had been improper. I said I liked his brand of impropriety – don't think he liked that too much because he left right after; said he had a plane to catch. Wished he'd stayed longer. A weekend of that impropriety would have been fantastic. I asked if he would write and he grunted something. We'll see what happens.*

The next entry that mentioned Hilaire was dated 5th April, six weeks later.

> *Sent a letter to Hilaire the week after he left and sent two others since then. It's over a month since I sent the first one and he hasn't replied. I sent another one yesterday to let him know that I still have fond memories of our time together. Would be nice if he kept in touch.*

She skimmed through later entries, looking out for the name Hilaire. An entry on September 29th caught her attention; she read:

Fine kettle of fish I've cooked for myself. No response from Hilaire to any of the letters I've sent him. Guess I was an idiot to expect otherwise. I'll stop writing for a while. Maybe my silence will make him wonder what has happened and he'll write. I won't tell him about this. I'll just wait and see what happens. When he finds out, he'll want to get in touch. For now, I'm in this on my own, though.

The next relevant entry was dated 19th January 1947. She read:

New year; new life – definitely with this little one. What a wonderful Christmas gift. Alert from Day 1; bright eyes . . . he'll be as intelligent as his father; looks exactly like him. I'll give him his name. He'll be a surprise to Hilaire when he comes for the next training session in March. I won't say anything till then. I'll just invite him over and he'll see this wonderful little surprise.

The rest of the entry contained details about the child and her maternal feelings. The final entry that had any reference to Hilaire was dated 13th April 1947. She read:

Well he didn't turn up. When I checked the training office the coordinator said that he had declined the offer. I've been blaming myself. Maybe if I'd told him he would have come. Then I've been thinking if he was interested at all he would have come anyway. Gone through enough ifs and maybes. Yesterday I sent him a note to tell him. Sent a copy of the birth certificate and some photos too. Explained that I kept it a secret to surprise him when he got here for training. The news must certainly make him want to visit. We'll see.

The last few entries did not mention Hilaire at all. She was hoping to find something more, something definitive and final although she was already convinced that Hilaire Charlemagne was her brother. She slipped her hand into the pocket inside the back cover just to be sure there was nothing there. As she pulled her hand out, a corner of a page stuck out beyond the edge of the fold of the pocket. She pulled it out. It was a yellowing sheet that was folded in two. She opened it and there was one paragraph of handwriting in fading black ink. She read:

Dear Madge, I am sorry you had to face this situation on your own. You should have said something before now. I don't know that I could have made things better or can even now because there is no future with me that I can offer. I'm married and I was sure I had told you when we met. I accept what you say that this is my son. I received the birth certificate and thank you for the photos. I'm sorry things got out of hand at your party. I also regret the difficulty that you must now be experiencing. I am enclosing some money to help with the costs you must have already incurred. I will send you some more when I can. Please accept my apology and I hope you understand my situation which doesn't allow me to offer you any comfort. I hope you will find happiness with someone more worthy. Hilaire.

The handwriting on the note had the same slant as her father's. She was sure now that she had read the entries and the note that Hilaire Charlemagne was her brother. She had discovered what must have been written on the second torn page of her father's journal. Her mother probably had not known or she would have mentioned it. She would have wanted Dawn to know that there was a male out there who was related to her. She also would not have been happy finding out yet another incident of infidelity and she would have shown some signs of her displeasure. Dawn remembered how upset she had been when Charlemagne St Ange had turned up to visit out of the blue and announced that he was Hilaire's son. A second revelation would have made her bitter. She was gone now and Dawn was relieved that she had been spared that. A wave of resentment bubbled up as she thought about her mother and her father's deception.

Garnet would need to know that he had another brother. And there was Charlemagne Joy who didn't know he had another brother on another island. She leaned back, thinking about complications that could arise later if siblings were unaware of each other's existence. She sighed. She would call Hilaire later to let him know what she had found out and then she would have to tell Garnet. One of them would have to tell Charlemagne Joy.

She sighed again. Perhaps one day they might be together and there might be joy but she didn't feel any in this moment. She opened her father's journal, turned to a blank page and began to write what she now knew he must have written on the second torn page.

Dear Departed

Albertina Toussaint walked along the narrow path between the rows of graves in the cemetery. She smiled, thinking that the cemetery was set out almost like the streets of the city with the paths crossing each other and creating distinct blocks. The next block over from where she stood would take her to the row with Cyril's grave. She muttered as she walked. It's like walking from Grass Street to Mary Ann Street and just like how our houses used to be. Ours on Grass Street and his on Mary Ann Street. She pursed her lips as she remembered Cyril. I will leave a candle for you so you can rest in peace. She walked towards the row with Cyril's grave. It was All Souls Day and the cemetery was aglow with the flickering flames of candles and small battery-operated lamps that families and friends had placed on the graves of their loved ones. Albertina stopped and checked the bag which she held in one hand and which contained candles, two small vases, bottles and a box of matches. In her other hand she clutched a few bunches of flowers which had already started to wilt. She closed the bag and continued along the path. I didn't forget nothing this time. I going to Cyril first. After all, he was my husband. Even though I didn't see him for most of the years we married.

She walked between two graves, sat down on one and placed her bags on it. She was short of breath. After a while she opened the bag, took out a vase, put a bunch of flowers in it and poured some water from one of the bottles in the bag. Look what nice flowers I bring for you, Cyril. I bring some pink roses because you used to like them and some ferns to finish the bouquet. I sure that will make you happy. This year I bring a lamp with a shade. It have batteries so it will continue to light when the candle burn down. You getting one candle and one lamp. I sure you will like that too. She lit the candle and turned on the lamp. She stood up and tilted her head to one side. The grave looking real nice, you know. See how it paint up and your name clear on the headstone. I sure that making you happy. I wish all this happiness was there before you get here though. We didn't even have a chance to talk before you get here. Eh eh! They bring you home in a box, a big present for me, cold like ice, not a word and I there waiting for you to walk in the door. That wasn't nice. She took another bottle from the bag, unscrewed the top and took a swig from the bottle. She wiped her mouth with the back of her hand, took another swig, screwed the cap on and put the bottle back in the bag. That is what keep me warm all these years, you know; that and Alphonse. Don't get vex now. Is you who leave me. I sit down waiting, my face getting gwiji, crease up like a ole prune. What's that you say? Listen, I not getting in any long talk now, you hear? Look how the place pretty. Look how your grave light up and nice. Rest in peace, you hear? I goin round by Alphonse grave to put some flowers for him. I sure his children leave already so I can go and put a little remembrance for him too. You don't have to get vex. What's that you say? Pa alé? Don't go? Why I must not go? Like you talking to me all de time now? Your voice runnin in my head like the rara duh children start to make already for Christmas. Listen, you is dust in there, you know. But see how the flowers looking nice in the light. I going now, you hear?"

She gathered the other flowers, picked up her bag and set off slowly down the row. It getting late, you know. I had to wait until Alphonse children left because I ain't want to meet them here. I will put a light and flowers for him. They ent going come back here for another year, so they ent going know who put them there. Everything will be gone by next year except the candle wax and they not going remember what they put here for him. Cyril mus be blue vex because I putting flowers and candle for Alphonse. But why he have to be vex? He die well before Alphonse come by me. Sa pou fè? What to do? She walked up to a grave which had two lighted lamps and a couple wreaths on it. My, my! They treat you nice this year; they treat you real nice but I suppose one lamp and one wreath is for you and the other ones is for your madam. I sure she won't mind if I put this little bunch of flower and a candle for you. I have to tell you thanks but I sorry for the shame too. She placed the vase with the flowers between the wreaths, lit a candle, made the sign of the cross and turned away. Madam, don be vex; I praying for you . . . what's dat you say, Alphonse? I sure I hear you say it don't matter just like you use to tell me. It don matter? The priest tell me I must pray for her too so I doin that, and I was jus' telling she about that when you interrupt me. Look how nice my flowers and candle looking right there between your wreath and she own. She reached into the bag, took out the small flask, unscrewed the cap and took a long drink.

It cold here, you know, even with all these lights I feeling cold right in my stomach. She started to walk away, then stopped and turned back to look at the grave. What you say, Alphonse? Stay? I stay long enough already. The madam ain't goin like it if I sit down on duh grave talking with you and she inside there too. Same like I hearing you, she mus be hearing everyting we saying. I feel enough shame for you already so I goin now. She mumbled and gesticulated as she walked towards the entrance of the cemetery. She felt a hand on her shoulder and cried out "Bon Dyé." She turned round quickly.

"My God, you make me jump. I didn' hear you."

"Miss Albertina, you okay?" Her neighbour, Juliana, was peering at her with a worried look. "I saw you talking and waving your hands as though something was bothering you."

"Is nothing, Julie; sé pa anyen. I okay. Is jus' my head full up . . . they talking to me all de time . . . telling me all sorta tings. Is nothing."

"Who? Who talking to you?" Juliana looked around then back at Albertina. "Who telling you what?"

Albertina pushed up her glasses from the tip of her nose and stared at Juliana. "Never mind, you wouldn understand."

"I can give you a lift if you want. The car is parked over there. I have to make one quick stop and I'll be back in a few minutes."

"Thanks, I'll wait for you." Albertina walked slowly towards the cars parked at the entrance. Don bother follow me, you hear? Go back; is here you belong.

Juliana dropped her off at her house and watched as Albertina went inside. The house remained dark for a long while and she thought to follow Albertina to make sure she was fine, but just as she was about to turn off the engine a light came on inside and she drove off.

Albertina sat at the small kitchen table. Her shoulders were hunched, her elbows propped on the table and she cradled her head in the palms of her hands. The naked bulb at the end of a long cord hanging from the ceiling cast a glow on a covered shoebox on the table in front of her. She looked up, reached for the flask next to the box, drank from it and shook her head. No, I say no, is not me who cause all dat. Is not me, is Cyril. She removed the lid from the box and took out a dried spray of flowers. The jasmine still smelling sweet. They still here, sweet like when Cy did give me. She reached into the box and picked up a bundle of letters tied together with a faded red ribbon. She took out another bundle tied loosely with a blue ribbon, then she reached in and took out a single envelope. She ran her finger along the top edge and placed it next to the two bundles on the table. She untied the ribbon from the first bundle and spread the letters in front of her. She picked up one, pulled out a couple sheets of paper from the envelope, held them up to the light, pushed her glasses up from the tip of her nose and started to read. Every now and then she read aloud:

> I must tell you, Tina, this place not the best to live. You wouldn't like it. Is like a camp. The house I living in have only one bedroom and a small kitchen and bathroom. I know if you was here that would be a paradise for me, but I out every day, for most of the day and you wouldn't like that. Is a place for people to work and then leave when the work finish. That's what I will do, my dear. Soon as I make enough money to buy a bigger house, I will leave here and come home. I does think about you all the time, I really missing you. I can't wait to come back. Your one true love, Cy.

She hummed softly as she folded the letter and put it back in the envelope. She stopped humming, tilted her head sharply to the left, a slight frown on her brow. What you say, Cy? You still love me? Is now you telling me? Why you didn' take me with you? Why you didn' come back sooner, eh? Why? She reached for the flask and took a long drink. Ahh; dat warm me up. Don't bother me, Cy. Not because I reading your letters you must think you should come to bother me. You hear what I tell you? You leave me and gone, what you expect? Is not me to blame, you hear? She picked up another letter, pushed her glasses up from the tip of her nose and started to read:

> My Tina, your letter arrived safely and I read it over and over. I miss you too, my dear, and I will come home soon, don't you worry. The girl who does come to clean the house saw me holding your letter to my heart and she tell me she wish she had somebody to love her like that. Did I tell you? The company send somebody to come and clean for us. Lena is the person cleaning. I will tell you more the next time I write. Take care of you for me till I come home. Your one love, Cy.

Albertina folded the letter, put it back in the envelope and placed it on the table. Cy, is this Lena why you decide to stay over there, not so? I know everything now, even if you didn' write it out, Cy. I shoulda listen to my mind and go over there right after I get this letter. What's dat you say? It wasn't necessary? It was well necessary, you hear? But like they say, hindsight is twenty-twenty vision. She pulled the second bundle of letters towards her, took one out close to the bottom of the bundle, smoothed out the single sheet and read:

> Dear Tina, you don't know how sorry I am I could not come for Christmas. I know you saying I broke my promise, but they had a big order to fill and the Manager ask some of us to work over the holidays. He say they would pay us double so I stay because of the extra I could make. I almost have enough for us to buy a new house. I already send a little money for you to put in the bank. Write and tell me when you get it. Is real hard working in the oilfield, Tina. They had us out there all day long over the holidays. The Manager give a party for us at the end of the work. It wasn't bad, it had dancing and everything. I learn how to dance the merengue – I will teach you when I come home. Lena, the girl

who does the cleaning, show me how to dance it. I buy a few 45s to bring home.
We will dance and have a good time. Take care of yourself and we will see each
other soon. Your Cy.

Albertina put the letter back in the envelope. If it was only merengue
you was dancing, Cy. If is only merengue things would be different. Is
not what I thinking? What it was, then? Tell me. What make you stay
longer and longer before you send me a letter, eh? I use to get one every
two weeks and after the holidays and the dancing I only hearing from
you every two months. What is that, eh? Is the merengue and the other
dancing you start to do, Cy. That's what it was. But how a man can be so,
eh? She sighed, picked up the last letter in the second bundle, opened it
and started to read.

> *Dear Tina, I writing to let you know I coming home. I book a passage on the*
> *Lady Joy and it leaving here the first of the month. I will be home a week after*
> *that. I coming home. Things getting a little complicated over here and I have to*
> *come home to clear my head and see you again. I make enough money for now.*
> *I will teach you to dance the merengue. We will have a party and a nice time,*
> *Tina. I want to see you again and I coming home in two weeks. Take care till I*
> *come, you hear? Cyril*

Albertina covered her face with her hands and rocked from side to side,
humming softly. She lifted her head and tilted it to one side as though
listening. It wasn't your fault? Not your fault? Whose fault it was, Cy? Is
not me who make you change your mind. Not me. Why you had to cancel
your ticket to come home? Imagine! The *Lady Joy* sail in and I there on the
wharf dress up like a Christmas tree and waiting for you to come down.
How you think I feel when they tell me you cancel your ticket? Eh? How
you think I feel? And is not even you who tell me. You don't even write
to tell me you cancelling duh ticket. I don't know why you do that, Cy.
What you say? You didn't cancel it, you just postpone it? For what? Miss
Lena didn't want you to leave, Cy? Don't tell me not to say that because
I saying it. I saying it because it true. What difference it make? Cancel
or postpone you still ain't come and when two months pass I still ain't
hear from you and is your coffin dat arrive later. I hear Miss Lena say

you was dancing when you get a heart attack. Is merengue or what Cy? Is in de bed you was dancing? What I hear again is something you eat dat give you bad indigestion and bring on de heart attack. Is something she cook for you, Cy? She cook for you so she could keep you, not so? She picked up the last letter from the table, took out a cable gram and another sheet of paper. She opened the cable: CYRIL FELL ILL LAST NIGHT STOP DID NOT RECOVER STOP LETTER FOLLOWS STOP.

She drank from the flask on the table, opened the other sheet of paper and read:

Dear Mrs Toussaint, It is with sadness that we write to inform you of the sudden death of Mr Cyril Toussaint. He suffered a heart attack a few days before he was due to leave. An ambulance was called as soon as his helper reported that he was ill, but the doctors were not able to revive him. We will be sending his body home and we will let you know of the arrangements we will be making to send his belongings. Please accept our condolences. Yours sincerely, Andre Valdez, Manager.

She reached for the flask, took a drink and folded the letter. Is you drive me to this, Cy, is you. Alphonse help me forget. I don't know why you talking to me anyway, making me read your letters to bring all this up again. I not going to do this again, you hear? Why you even talking to me, I don know. Go back, Cy, go back to your grave and leave me alone. I gone through enough already. Maybe is de letters I keep for so long and reading once a year that making you think you can talk to me. You don't have to explain nothing, you hear? You six feet deep and is there you staying. Is enough now. I going burn the letters so I don't have to go back on these things. What you say? No, I ain't going forget you. I will put flowers and a candle for you every November, on All Souls Day so you will rest in peace. But I not going to have conversation with you again, you hear? Is time for you to leave me, Cy.

She took another drink from the bottle, gathered the pile of letters, took a coal pot from under the kitchen sink, put the letters in it and poured rum from her bottle on the pile. She held up one sheet, lit a match, dropped it in the coal pot and smiled. She sat down, took another drink and started to hum and sway as she watched the letters go up in flames. She wiped tears from her cheek, rested her head on her arms and fell asleep.

※

There was a knock on the kitchen door. Albertina closed the tap, wiped her hands on her apron and went quickly to open the door. Her husband's friend, Alphonse, stood there. "Alphonse, is you! When you come back?"

"Morning, Bertina. I got back two days ago but I couldn't come to see you right away. So many things to settle. But I had to come because I know how bad you must be feeling about Cyril."

"You can say that again. Come in, Alphonse. I was making breakfast, saltfish with cucumber souse, and bakes. I have avocado too. You want some?"

"Thanks, Bertina; I won't say no to that."

They sat at the table. Albertina smiled as she watched Alphonse wolf down his food.

"This is good, you know. Over there in the oilfield canteen they served fish every day and sometimes chicken, but never saltfish like how we make it here. And the food wasn't highly season so you could taste the freshness of the fish. Cyril use to say they take it from the sea and throw it straight in the pot. After a while he stop eating the canteen food. He say, after your good cooking he couldn't digest that." They laughed.

"At least he remember something good I use to do. So where he use to eat, then?"

Alphonse paused, looked down at his plate, then looked up at Albertina. He reached out and put his hand over hers.

"Bertina, life was hard over there, real hard. Cyril was missing you bad. A day wouldn't pass without him saying how he miss you and wish he could go home."

"At first, yes, Alphonse. I believe that because he use to say it in his letters. But after a while is like he forget and the letters get cold, like he draw away from me. I sure you notice something too, but you ain't going tell me. You his friend. Where you say he was eating?"

"He pay the cleaner, Lena, to cook. He give her extra to prepare a meal for him once or twice a week and other times he cook for himself."

"So she did take over for true."

"Don't fret yourself, Bertina. It don't matter now. She never move in duh house with Cyril. I never see her living there. She use to cook and I know Cyril appreciate the little she use to do."

"You all the same. Even now you covering up for Cyril. You think I don't know? Long time I suspect he had something with this Lena. He write and tell me things was getting complicated so he coming home. I believe he get in deep with she and then he decide he should leave but he cancel the trip and next thing you know, he dead. You know what happen, Alphonse, but you not goin to tell me."

"I know how you feeling, Bertina. I know is hard, but I will tell you. Lena get close to Cyril and he tell me she want him to marry her. That's when he decide to leave and come back home. Cyril couldn't carry on with that and go on like you didn't exist. He tell Lena that he was married and he had to come home to settle things. He say he didn't tell her more because you never know what could happen. He tell me he was making preparations to leave the company for good, but he didn't tell Lena that. All of that must be the complications he tell you about. Anyway, is hard to keep secret in a place like that. I think Lena must hear Cyril don't plan to return to the company."

"So is obeah she put on him to make him change his mind? Why he didn't come on the *Lady Joy* like he plan to do?"

"I don't know, Bertina. He say he had to clear up his business and he wouldn't have time to make it on the *Lady Joy* but he was planning to leave on the next boat that come in. He tell me that and I believe him. But you know what happen."

"Yes, I know. If is true is heart attack he did have, then is break his heart break to leave this Lena. I sure she put obeah on him."

"Cyril make up his mind to come home and because he know he leaving for good he say he will have a cook-up and some drinks for all ah we before he leave. He say Lena offer to cook. I remember that night well. We eat and drink and have a good time, but I find it strange she give him his plate of food special. She bring it from the kitchen and give it to him. He wink at me and he eat it all up. I stay with him for a bit after the others leave and Lena say she have something to do so she going but she will return to clean up. I left when she get back. I was just going to bed when I hear a knocking on the door and is Lena there telling me come quick because Cyril pass out. When I go over there, I see Cyril on the bed; he ain't moving and he sweating. I tell Lena call for help and the ambulance came and take him to the hospital but they say he dead by the time he get there. They say it look like he did have a heart attack but I don't know what bring that on. You ask me, Bertina, so I telling you like how it happen."

"Cyril was a sweet man. I sure Lena didn't want him to leave. If is obeah she do, must be one of dem potions they does sell that she give him. People does buy them because of the name but who know what they put in the bottle? I hear it have one they calling 'Man-U Must' and another one 'Leave Me Never'. Must be one of them she give him."

Alphonse stood up and placed his hands on her shoulders. "I don't know, Bertina. You can call on me anytime if you need help. I know how hard this must be for you. I will come by to visit to make sure things okay."

He left and Albertina continued with her life of aloneness, thinking about the circumstances Cyril faced and embellishing the story Alphonse told her to her satisfaction. She made it a ritual to go to the cemetery on All Souls Day to place flowers on his grave and light a candle. Alphonse dropped by to see her occasionally at first; then on his way back from his early morning walks, he would call out to her and she would shout an acknowledgement from wherever she was in the house. As this became something of a routine, she decided to sit by the window in the front room so they would not have to shout. He would pause by the window to ask her how she was getting on and they would talk about this and that. The pauses became visits in the front room, then coffee at the kitchen table. The friendly arm around her shoulders as he left became affectionate hugs, and one morning the rain began to pour as he was about to leave and the hug turned into an embrace that left them clinging to each other and surrendering to a passion that left Albertina sighing as she struggled to fasten the buttons on her blouse while Alphonse pulled on his sneakers and ran out into the rain.

She did not see him for two weeks, during which time she vowed never to let herself get in such a situation again, even as she flushed with pleasure at the memory of Alphonse swearing love for her as his lips and hands found every erogenous spot on her body. Then one morning as she lay in her bed before dawn, she heard a tapping on the kitchen door. There was Alphonse in his running clothes on his way out for his walk.

"I had to come, Bertina."

She opened the door and without a word she held his hand and led him to her still warm bed. So their affair began in earnest. They never mentioned Marie, Alphonse's wife. It was as if they alone existed in this pre-dawn world. This went on for months and Albertina's reliance on her favourite rum diminished a little. She allowed herself a ti ponche – the local spiced rum aperitif – before lunch every day and another one or two in the evening before going to bed. Alphonse's presence in her life and his lovemaking, though limited to the early morning visits, gave her a new lease on life and the feeling that she was needed and loved.

She was surprised one afternoon when she heard his familiar knock on her kitchen door. She opened the door and he slipped in and pulled the door shut, looking furtively behind him as he did so.

"What happen, Alphonse?"

He pulled a chair and sat at the kitchen table.

"I didn't want to stand at your front door in the middle of the day, Bertina. I think people talking enough already."

"What you mean? Who talking?"

"Marie tell me how somebody tell her I coming here in the morning. She say I making a pappyshow and a bétise with she life. She say the neighbours looking at her and laughing and she not going to let nobody make her look like a fool and a nonsense."

"Bon Dyé! My God, is so people like to bad talk, eh? What you tell her?"

"What you think I can say? It don't matter. I didn't answer. I just shake my head as if to say all dat is stupidness. But I make up my mind to go away for a little while, let things cool down a little. I going country by my sister. That's what I come to tell you."

"When you going?"

"Saturday. Day after tomorrow. I taking the early bus. Is a long drive. But I will come tomorrow morning as usual to say goodbye."

The next morning he came through the yard and she opened the kitchen door to let him in. She closed the door as he entered, reached for his hand and led him directly into her room. Neither said a word. They clung to each other and Albertina moved with a vigour she had not shown in the year they had been together. Alphonse was gasping intermittently, but she was carried away by a surge of passion which was more intense because he would be leaving. Over the heavy thud of her heartbeat she heard Alphonse call "Bertina!" in a muffled voice, then she felt his dead weight against her body.

Albertina was nowhere to be found later when a small group gathered in front of her house. Marie, Alphonse's wife, had entered and after an hour or so a hearse arrived and two attendants went in and emerged shortly afterwards carrying a body wrapped in a sheet on a stretcher. Marie followed them holding a pair of sneakers in her hands. Her mouth was set in a thin line as she watched them put the body into the hearse. As the hearse drove away she turned, walked down the sidewalk and entered her house a few doors away.

On the day after the funeral Albertina was seen approaching her house in the opposite direction from Alphonse's house and she was gesticulating as though in conversation but there was no one with her. There were rumours that she had fled to the country, that she had locked herself in an outhouse in her yard, but no one knew for sure where she had gone the morning Alphonse spilled his dying love over her. Now she always approached her house via a roundabout route, so she avoided walking in front of Alphonse's house. It was clear that she had changed since the events of that morning.

Albertina slowly raised her head. A shaft of sunlight fell on the ribbons that had bound the letters from Cyril. The smell of smoke from the burnt letters hung in the kitchen. She wiped her eyes and picked up the ribbons. It finish now, Cyril. I don't have the letters and I don't have to listen to you. She tilted her head to one side. All she heard was the wind whistling through the wooden louvres of the window. She smiled, got up, shut the louvres, picked up the ribbons and threw them into the garbage. She picked up the flask from the table, shook it and put it back down. Empty. But I okay for now. She turned off the kitchen light, looked around and smiled. Is just like when Alphonse use to come.

As she turned to make her way to her room she stopped and tilted her head towards the kitchen door. Is who that so early this morning? She went to the door, opened it and held out her hand. She closed the door, a broad smile on her face. Is really you? Come in, my dear.

Imogene

Moise sat on the rock, his fishing line trailing beneath the surface of the water. The sea was calm this morning but he had caught nothing, although he had been sitting out since four thirty. This was his favourite time to fish because the beach was usually empty. The fish would be on or just beyond the reef, foraging for an early feed. Later, he would take his rod, net and the pail with whatever he had caught and leave them under a nearby sea grape tree while he went in for a swim. A faint light was slowly creeping over the brow of the hills in the east. He heard a laugh, like a tinkle, a happy sound. He thought of the word "tinkle" because it was a clear sound, like that of a bell he could hear when he passed in front of the church on his way home around seven. He turned around to where the sound came from. A couple emerged from the stand of sea grapes lining the beach. The young woman was laughing as she ran ahead of the man. She was twirling, leaping and spinning across the sand. Moise could tell she was a dancer. The man followed with a lumbering gait. He stopped and watched her, a smile on his face.

"Such grace! I would say, grace and beauty in motion." He applauded. She twirled, leaped, twirled again, her arms above her head, and curtsied in front of him.

"For a writer you are prone to using clichés." She reached up, pressed her palms against his chest and turned her face up to his. He cupped her face in his hands and deliberately kissed her forehead, eyes, nose, each cheek and then her lips. "You are my never hackneyed, never overused, ever renewing cliché, so I can rediscover the unfolding wonder of who you are." She spun away from him, laughing.

"That's a contradiction." She pulled off her wrap, danced to the water and dived in, her body arching above a breaking wave. He shed his clothes and followed, walking into the surf, his legs pushing against the waves. She had surfaced and was looking at him, a broad smile on her face.

"Just dive in, you won't notice the cold then." She scooped some water in her hands and threw it in his direction. He plunged beneath a wave and surfaced beside her, his arms held stiffly at his sides. She laughed, a prolonged tinkling that made Moise smile. They swam out together.

As Moise walked along the beach, he noticed their clothes thrown carelessly above the water line, and their shoes, slip-on sandals, set neatly side by side in front of the pile. He nodded, smiled and made his way further down the beach to have his swim.

The Mother

"Imogene." Her mother turned towards her from the stove. "You seem very happy these days. If I didn't know better, I'd say you're in love. What's up?"

Imogene laughed.

"I've met someone rather nice. I met him at the creative writing workshop."

"How's that going? Are you finding it useful?"

"It's great, Mother, and I'm learning new stuff. The people are interesting."

"So who is this interesting person you've met? Is it someone I know?"

"I don't think so. At least, I've never heard you or Dad mention him or his family."

"So who is he?"

"He's a writer, and a brilliant one. At least, I think so. He works for one of the local newspapers. The one you call a scandal sheet."

"If he is one of those writing or contributing to the articles in that rag, then I'm not sure how brilliant . . ."

"Don't be like that, Mother. See? You're already beginning to think badly of him. He needs a job so he works with that paper. That's where he got the job, but he's a novelist and he's just finished his first novel. It's brilliant. I read some of it."

"I see. So you've been seeing each other for a while, then."

"Only since the workshop started. He read some of his work there and because I asked so many questions, he offered to let me read some more of it. We met a few times outside the workshop."

"You don't know much about this person, do you? You're so impulsive. What did you say his name is?"

"I didn't tell you yet. It's Grant. Grant St Esprit."

"Oh! I know the St Esprits. They live at Vigie, don't they? I sometimes see Mrs St Esprit in church."

"No, Mother. His family doesn't live there. He and his mother live in the Conway. I don't think there's a relationship . . ."

"Goodness! The Conway! That's a slum area."

"Well, his mother raised him on her own and he lives with her there. His dream is that his writing will make him well off so they can move out of there."

"Well, you need to be careful, Imogene. You never can tell with these . . . with . . . with people."

"See what I mean? I bet if I said he was from Vigie or Cap Estate you wouldn't have a problem or said what you just said."

"I don't have a problem, child; and I'm just cautioning you so you don't end up with one. You're only seventeen. How old is this Grant, anyway?"

"He's thirty."

"Almost twice your age! And more experienced, I bet. You're probably a moth to his flame. And you're smitten."

"You're making a drama of this, Mother. He's a nice person. Anyway, I feel more like a butterfly than a moth when I'm with him. He makes me laugh and I feel like dancing. Maybe I'll take up dancing as a career. What do you think?"

"Well, you're good at it and I know you like it. But your father will probably object. He'd say it's a career with a short life. No sustainability."

"Not if I become a professional and prosperous dancer. Anyway, I'm not sure, so don't tell him anything."

"I'll have to mention St Esprit if he asks what you're up to. These days you're rarely here when he comes home and if he asks, I won't cover up for you."

"There's nothing to cover up, Mother."

"Be careful, anyway. I hope this Grant has been granted the saintly spirit he needs to treat you well."

Imogene chuckled. "That's funny. You translated the good things in his name. 'Saintly spirit' and he does have a good spirit. One of these days I'll bring him over to meet you and Dad."

The Beach

Moise cast his net. There was a school of minnows in the shallows and he could see another school of twi twi beyond the lip of the reef. If he could catch most of them he would have a good sale because the housewives always asked him about twi twi. They were the best for making fishcakes. He heard the tinkling laughter, turned around and saw the couple, arms entwined, looking at him. The girl greeted him with a musical "good morning" which he acknowledged with a nod and a wave of his hand. They left their sandals, side by side above the high water mark, where the sand was loose and blown about in eddies by the wind. They walked down the beach.

"We don't see enough of each other since the workshop ended," he complained.

"What?" She laughed. "Didn't we see each other just the night before last?"

"Just what I mean. It isn't every day." He pulled her closer to his side. "I have good news."

"What? Tell me."

"Remember when the workshop started Mr Lee suggested that I send my manuscript for publication and submit it for the London Academy fiction competition? Well . . . the publishers accepted it and it will be out later this year. Aaaand, guess what? They're offering me a contract for a second novel."

"I'm impressed. Now you can write full time and not have to worry about 'earning pennies'. So are you going to give up your penny job?"

"I can't yet. Don't know if I'll be able to depend on income from the book. At least the offer of the advance for the next book is generous so I can work part time and spend more time writing. I haven't heard anything yet about the competition."

"Your mother must be happy."

"You know her, she looked up to heaven, lifted her arms and said 'Mèsi Bon Dyé. God, you answer my prayers.' And she went on in a paean to God in French Creole."

"Oh, I wish I'd heard her. French Creole is musical. I'm learning it."

"Really? Don't you know it already?"

"No. My parents didn't speak it to me when I was small, even though they both speak it. They switched to it when they didn't want me to understand what they were saying."

"You poor thing! Deprived of a fundamental part of your culture! Not to worry, I'll speak it with you so you'll learn faster. I'll teach you many things."

"Deprived? Says who? Bet you can't do this!" She pulled away from him, twirled, and humming a local tune, she stepped delicately across the sand. "This is the La Commette, one of our folk dances. Bet you can't do it. Who's deprived?" She laughed. "Race you back to the cove. Last one in is deprived." She ran down the beach.

Moise looked up and smiled at the image of Imogene sprinting, curls of her Afro windswept, while the man lumbered behind her, some distance away. She tossed her wrap in the direction of the shoes, ran towards the sea and dived, a clean arc into the incoming wave.

The Father

Imogene's father looked up when she rushed into the kitchen and sat at the table.

"Sorry I'm late. Went for an early swim." She reached for one of the mangoes in the bowl on the table.

"I see you're making these early morning swims a habit, Genie. It will keep you healthy." Her father sipped his coffee and looked at her over the rim of his cup. "I notice you set off while it's still dark. Be careful."

"Exactly what I've been telling her," her mother chimed in. "Coming in late and going out again before the crack of dawn. Burning her candle at both ends; that's what she's doing."

"It's a long way to the beach and I like to get back before the sun's too hot. It's great exercise walking to the beach and swimming. See how fit I am?" She got up and spun around. Her father smiled.

"Good idea to have some company."

"Yeah, I'm doing that. My friend Grant goes along too."

Her mother placed a plate of eggs in front of her father and sat down. "George, I guess you've noticed this is a new fad. It only started when Mr Grant-in-Aid came along."

George paused, the fork midway to his mouth. "Does that mean you don't approve?"

"Approve? Me? How can I approve? I've never met this person. All I know is that he lives in some corner of town. Imogene seems to be completely taken up with him."

"He's very nice, Dad. We met at the workshop and he's a soon-to-be-famous novelist."

"Interesting. I'd like to meet him sometime."

"Sure thing. He works long hours but I'm sure we can arrange something."

"Do you know anyone from Conway, George? That's where he lives."

"Mildred, you know I meet people from all over in my line of work. Of course I do."

"But do you know the St Esprit family? From what I gather it's a two-person family. He lives with his mother."

"Don't think I know them. I would remember. But I'd like to meet them. I look forward to it, Genie. Gotta go, it's getting late." He kissed his wife's forehead, returned his daughter's high-five and left.

"As I was saying, Imogene. You need to be careful. First of all, it isn't seemly for a young lady to go walking to the beach with a man before it's light. What will people think?"

"Not again, Mother. Please. People aren't waking up at that hour of the morning to spy on anyone, let alone me."

"You never know who might be around. It's just not proper."

"That's so old school, Mother. Who cares?"

"I certainly do, and I don't want our name and your reputation dragged through the mud because of some silly flirtation. Think of your future."

"I am. Just let it be, please? I'm sure you'll like Grant once you meet him."

"We'll see. Just take care."

"Don't worry. Got to go." She was up and out through the door before her mother could get another word out.

The Harbour

"Miss G. Nice of you to come see me. Grant not here, you know."

"I came to see you, Miss Rose. Not Grant. He told me you were sick. How you feeling now?"

"Better, child, better. Look how much work I do already this morning." She gestured towards the table on which there were trays of turnovers and pastry puffs with custard inside.

"You made chou-a-la-crème. Yours are the best."

"I know you like them. Here, take one. If you like, I will show you how to make them."

"I'd like that. Then I'll be able to make them for Grant sometimes."

"I sure if you make it, he will eat it." She untied her apron and sat in the chair across from Imogene.

"This morning he leave in a hurry. I never see him so excited. He get a letter and he say he win the prize. I think he was going by you to tell you. You didn't see him yet?"

"No, not yet. Sunday was the last day I saw him when we went to the beach. That's when he told me you have the flu. You sure you better now?"

"Yes, child. Today I feeling good, and I happy for Grant too. These days all he talking about is leaving here. Now he going away, I will stay right here. This was my mother's house, you know. Her spirit still here." She turned her head and looked towards the harbour. They sat silently while Imogene nibbled around the edges of the pastry puff.

"What happen, it not tasting good?"

"I like to leave the custard in the middle for last. It's delicious." See the *Grenville Lass* coming in? Must be with people on excursion from Martinique. Is a nice view, Miss Rose. Must be nice to wake up to see this every morning."

"Yes, is nice. I like the view. Only thing with here is when it rain a lot and the tide is high, the water does come right up in the drains and sometimes the yard does get flooded. They can fix that if they want, but is poor people living here so the government not doing nothing about it. Is only that would make me leave here. I like watching the sea and the boats coming in. Look, see the *Lady Joy* coming in now?"

Imogene licked custard from her fingers.

"Mmm. This chou is the best, Ms Rose."

"Thanks, Miss G. Grant say I should open a bakery but I getting too old for that now. Mr Amar does come and buy everything I make and sell it in his shop so I don't have to worry. Now Grant have to go away, is not now I going open a bakery."

"I sure he not going for long. Is just to collect his prize, not so? He'll come back soon and help you."

"I don't know Miss G. He so restless these days. He never use to complain about here before. Now nothing here good enough for him.

He calling it a hell hole. My mother take good care of this house. I glad I don't have to rent from nobody and I making a living. I don mind it but Grant keep saying we have to leave."

"Telling tales on me, Ma?" Grant's voice signalled his entry through the back door. "What are you telling Genie about me?" He pulled a stool next to Imogene's and put his arm around her.

"Only the things you haven't told me." Imogene laughed.

"Seems like an eon since I saw you. I planned to visit you but you beat me to it."

"I came to check on your Mom. Congrats. She gave me the good news."

"I wanted to tell you myself and surprise you. I have to leave next week for the awards ceremony."

"So soon. How long will you be gone for?"

"Not sure. I expect to meet with the publisher to discuss what's possible. If I can get a part time job there, I'd like to work on the second novel and submit it before I come back."

"That's going to be a long haul, then."

"Don't frown like that. It's just an idea. I want to accelerate things so I can find Ma another place to live. This is the pits. The government won't do anything so we have to get out under our own steam."

"Who knows? There's lots of talk about developing the harbour area so they might just clear this up and build a new housing complex somewhere else."

"Huh! If it's anything like the CDCs they have in the middle of town we won't be going there."

"They aren't that bad, you know. A friend of mine lives in one of the apartments. She says it's comfortable."

"Maybe she's been lucky to get one on the second floor. No elevators to the third or fourth floors. All those stairs to climb! My mother wouldn't make it halfway up. And the ground floor is a no-no. Everyone can look right into your house; no privacy. We need to find a better place." He leaned across and squeezed his mother's shoulder. "What you say, eh, Ma? He turned to Imogene. "It would be great if I could spend some extra time up there and write the second book. What I need is a sponsor."

Imogene frowned. "In this day and age? You mean a patron, don't you? You'd probably have to prostitute your talent or yourself for that. Give something to get something."

"So young and so cynical. The world's not as bad as you make it sound, Genie."

"You should talk! Didn't you just condemn this world we live in here?"

"Finding a sponsor . . ."

"A patron." She turned away from him and looked across the harbour.

"Okay, a patron, call it what you want. That's a different thing from trying to get out of a slum. If I had a sponsor . . ." He paused a moment, smiling at Imogene then turned away. "If I had a patron, I could concentrate on writing. I would do anything . . . anything; whatever it takes to give me the chance to get ahead. If I had to work part-time here or there it would take me forever to write the novel. Things are difficult here. There's nothing here for writers like me. There's no future."

Imogene grimaced. The sunlight on the water was blinding. She closed her eyes.

"How come you lookin so sad, Miss G?" Rose put a hand on her arm.

"Nothing much, Miss Rose; was just thinking." There was a long pause, then she turned to Grant. "Next week is just two days away. You'll soon be gone."

"The sea is gloriously calm these days. I have time for another early morning swim. How about tomorrow?"

"Tomorrow is good."

News

"You're going to have to find something to do, Imogene. You can't sit around all day moping."

Imogene turned the page of the newspaper she was reading. "I'm checking on stuff, Mother."

"At this stage it can't be anything strenuous. You've got to take care of yourself." She glanced at Imogene over her shoulder. "Did you hear that they are going to clear the Conway and put in government offices there? They will build a new housing complex in the Cedars area and offer the homes to the people in the Conway." Imogene did not answer. Mildred turned round and looked at her. "Does Mr Grant-in-Aid know this? You haven't mentioned him in a long while. Have you heard from him?"

"I wish you wouldn't call him that, Mother. He's probably busy trying to write his second book."

"I think the name suits him fine." Mildred turned back to what she had been doing in the sink. "It suits him just fine. He gave you a lot of aid, didn't he?"

"Mother, please. Not again."

"You need to see things as they are, Imogene. Have you told him? When is he coming back? He's been off on a jaunt for months now, and here you are, flaunting a pregnancy. How do you think we feel? I can imagine the talk around town. This is humiliating."

Imogene's hand slapped the table sharply as she turned the page of the paper.

"Mother, I'm not flaunting anything. Do you think this is easy for me? The last few months have been tough. It's bad enough that he's . . ."

Mildred interrupted. "It's not right, and it doesn't look good. Did he say when he's likely to come back? And don't be rude, Imogene. I know you're frustrated but you don't have to scrape the legs of the chair on the floor like that . . . Imogene?" She turned around but Imogene was no longer at the table. The pages of the newspaper were fluttering in the breeze from the open window.

Mildred muttered under her breath as she dried her hands and walked over to the table. She picked up the chair that had fallen and was about to close the paper when she saw the photograph and the byline above it: "Our Boy Grant Does It". She read the brief paragraph below the photograph. *Grant St Esprit impressed his audience at the launch of his award-winning novel. He read excerpts from it and from his second novel which, he says, is on the way. After the official ceremony and the reading, fans who purchased the novel queued to get his autograph. Here we see St Esprit (centre), Publisher's*

Representatives Clive Davis (left) and Gina Martin (second left), Event Hostess and Patron Florence Tufton (right). Mildred noticed Grant's left arm curled around Tufton's waist. She was leaning against him, her head tilted back and she was smiling up at him. She squinted to discern whether the slight glint on his left hand was a reflection or a ring on his finger. She couldn't tell, but she knew that the photo was the reason Imogene had left the room suddenly. She began to fold the paper but changed her mind and left it open at the page with the photograph so that George would be sure to see it when he came in.

The Sea

Moise sat on the rock, his fishing line trailing beneath the waves. The sea was choppy and every now and then he was splashed by the spray rising from the waves dashing against the rocks. He had caught nothing but one never knew when a school of fish might drift in towards the reef. A faint first light was in the east. He thought he heard laughter and he smiled in anticipation. He turned around to look at the stand of sea grapes from which they usually emerged but it was too dark there to make out anything. He turned back to his fishing. It was close to the time for low tides but the waves remained high and the surge heavy. He thought he would skip his swim because the undertow might be strong and unpredictable with the sea so choppy. It was soon light and the sky in the east was aglow with the sun, a large orange ball. He gathered his gear, stuffed the net and line into the pail, picked his way gingerly across the rocks and stepped on to the beach.

It was empty this morning. He walked towards the stand of sea grapes which he had named Lovers' Grove because of the impression the two young lovers had made on him when they used to emerge from there every morning. It was several months since he had last seen them and he wondered what had become of them. Then he thought he had heard her laughter above the pounding of the waves earlier but it wasn't the usual light-hearted tinkle; more like a forlorn cry. He looked around expectantly as he walked along. He must have been mistaken because there was no one in sight on the beach. He noticed a wrap lying carelessly on the sand next to a pair of lady's sandals. He looked around, saw no one; then his eyes were drawn to the footprints leading from the clothes towards the sea. The waves had washed over most of them, but some were discernible in the soft loose sand where the waves had not reached. The sandals and wrap looked like those the dancing girl used to leave on the high ground before entering the water.

He paused, looked at them and the footprints, then turned towards the sea. The beach was still empty but the tide had turned and the sea was now a large calm pond with low gentle waves sighing across the sand.

Boloms

The Two

He perched on one of the rocks on the cliff overlooking the village. It was dark but he could see the white caps of the waves as they raced to dash against the rocks below. He came to the promontory every morning before dawn when he discovered that she left her house around that time to walk along the beach. Sometimes she climbed the narrow path to the clifftop and would sit staring out to sea. He liked when she did that because he could see her clearly then; the slim lines of her figure revealing the results of her efforts to keep trim; and the tell-tale grey around her temples – signs that she was getting older, the dark velvety patch around her eye that he thought most attractive. He wondered whether she worried and if part of it could be about him, about what she had done to him before he could establish a bond with her. He had known from early that she was sometimes afraid because he could feel ripples of fear in the currents that washed over him and he heard it in the fast and heavy beating of her heart.

When she climbed to the clifftop she would sit on a rock or on the ground, and on occasion she would stretch her arms up to the sky or hold her head in both hands and rock backward and forward. When she did that, he guessed she was in some sort of pain and sometimes he got a twinge of satisfaction, thinking that the pain might be because of her regret for what she had done to him. This morning she didn't climb the path to the cliff but walked slowly along the beach from one end of the bay to the other. He was intent on following her every move when a voice close by startled him. He looked up at what he thought was an image of himself until she hopped to perch on another rock closer to his. He realized it was a she from her voice.

"Why do you come here every morning?"

"How do you know I come here every morning? I've never seen you here before."

"I come often enough; not every day but I see you here whenever I come."

She straightened her back and looked around. A wisp of hair on her head shivered in the wind. "What you looking at?"

"She's down there on the beach."

"Aha, muth be someone special." She raised her arm, put her hand over her eyes and looked down at the beach. "I don't see anyone."

"She's there all right and if you want to know, it's my mother."

"Oh! You suffering from separation blues?"

"And you're inquisitive, aren't you?"

"I'm not. I juth happen to know all about separation blues. I come here for the same reason as you."

He looked around.

"I don't see anyone else around here."

"No. That's becauth she walked into the sea some time ago. The waves took her far out and she never came back. But I can hear her sigh when the waves wash across the sand."

"Sorry."

"I don't need pity. There's enough of that and stories about the likes of us going around these days."

"I haven't heard."

"If you used to roam like me, you would hear. Do you know that in the town up north people have been flocking every night thisth week to see a play about three brothers? There's a character, a bolom, like us, in it."

"I know about the play. I stopped by three nights in a row just to see parts of it. I like the lofty language."

"Curious. I went every night juth to see the parts with the bolom. The actor is cool."

"The acting and the language."

"Everybody talking 'bout thisth play. Lath night they were speaking about it on the radio and they were talking 'bout boloms too. None of it made sense to me."

"What did they say?"

"They were praising the Walcott man who wrote the play. They said he'sth faithful to his culture by using sthories from the folk tradition in his work." He noticed that her light lisp became pronounced when she was animated.

"Well, what did they say about boloms?"

"Oh! They said he presented a true picture about boloms. Better than the two folktales that were in the paper last week. One of the sthories was about Chinese boloms. It said boloms are the souls of children who died before they were baptized. Their feet are turned backward, they wear oriental hats and they don't have eyes or ears; only a round mouth." She turned to face him. "Let me look at you. Where are your feet?"

He turned his back to her and looked down at the beach. "If you're a bolom why don't you look at your own feet?"

"If I could see them, I wouldn't ask."

"Well, you can see, so it's not true we don't have eyes."

"I guess so."

"What else did they say?"

"Oh! They said the person still didn't get it right because he said boloms are foetuses taken from the womb by a sorcerer who made them do his bidding and sometimes the sorcerer made them do bad things. That didn't make sense either."

He turned to look at her.

"I guess you could call a person who does that sorcerer, can't you? Who else but someone like a sorcerer would tear us away from our mothers?"

"That sthory said boloms are grotesque and they are sadists who are addicted to mischief. The man on the show said the Walcott man came closest to presenting the true bolom."

"At least he knows how we come into being. Did you hear what the bolom in the play said? '*A woman did me harm, / called herself mother, / The fear of her hatred, a cord round my throat.*'"

"Ooh! You remember what the bolom said!"

"It doesn't say much in the play, does it?"

"No, but what it says gives me hope."

"How so? It only describes what we are and our situation. Didn't you hear it? '*I am neither living nor dead. / A puny body, a misshapen head.*' It said if it had been born it '*would have known life, rain on my skin, sunlight on my forehead*'."

"But doesn't it get free in the play? It doesth something good for the mother and that releases it from limbo and it experiences life. That'sth cool; makes me have hope."

"I don't know. What does the bolom in the play do?"

"It thwarts the devil. I s'pose that's the sorcerer in the play; and it helps the mother of the three boys. Thath was enough to free it from limbo so it could experience life."

He turned to look at the woman on the beach. She was sitting on the sand staring out to sea. A soft orange glow spread along the horizon. He glided off his rock.

"I have to go now. The sun is about to come up." She slid off her rock and hopped to stand next to him.

"Where do you go when it'sth daylight?"

"There's a cave beneath the cliff. It goes far into the cliff. It's deep, dark and cool. I'm going there now. You can come if you like."

They floated to the edge of the cliff, glided down the side and disappeared into the mouth of the cave below.

Their Imagined Lives

He perched on a smooth rock, his back hunched and his head pulled into his shoulders. She was curled on her side in foetal position on an adjacent rock. She looked around.

"There aren't any bats. I like that." She sat up and turned to look at him.

"What do you do down here all day?"

"What is there to do? You know what this life is like. We can't survive in sunlight." He paused for a moment, sighed and said, "I think about the things I see when I roam at night. I imagine what she must be doing, what she would be doing if I were a part of her life. Mostly, I imagine what my life would have been like if I'd been born."

"I do that a lot too. What'sth your life like?"

He leaned his back against the rock. "Family. I imagine my family. My father, mother and me living together in our house by the sea. We would do things together. They would take me places. I would be at the centre of their lives and we would be happy."

"What else?"

"What do you mean?"

"Well, what about later on when you grow up?"

"I almost always think about when I'm young. I don't know much else to think about, but since I saw that play I've been thinking how cool it must be to use language like that man who wrote the play. I went back mostly to listen to the language . . . so perhaps if I'd got older I'd probably want to use language like that; be a writer or something."

"Ooh, that'sth funny becauth since I saw the play I think I would be an actress."

"You'd have a hard time with that lisp."

"Saysth who? If I was born, my soul wouldn't be trapped in this puny body and my head wouldn't be mithsshapen. I'd be whole and grow and I wouldn't have a lispth. Know what? I'd be an actress and a dancer. My mother was a dancer and she would teach me and other little girls to dance."

"Sorry I said that."

"Okay. I imagine my mother strong. She didn't care much about what people thought or said about her. She would have me as the centre of her life and we would be happy together. I wouldn't care that I didn't know who my father was becauth my mother would be everything and she would never let me feel deprived. She was proud and ignored the local gossip. But someone broke her heart. Know what? She was a fantastic dancer. Thath how I got to be a dancer. And I would be an actress too. I would get a part in the play – the part of the bolom. I would move and speak so the audience would be methmerized when I said lines like *'he shrieked with delight / when a mother strangled me / Before the world light . . . / I would have known life, rain on my skin, sunlight on my forehead'."*

He turned away from her.

"So you remember the words of the bolom too! All we both seem to know about our lives is bound up in a play we saw. An imagined life made up by a man. We are nothing. We live in limbo, between darkness and the edge of light. We can never be anything with our souls trapped in these clods of flesh; half-formed bodies. Your mother walked into the sea and it swallowed her. Mine sits gazing at the sea like a broken soul. If only it were true that we would be free if we could cross the edge of light!"

Light

It had got darker as night fell. They could hear the waves pounding on the rocks at the mouth of the cave. This meant the sea was rough. They floated up from their perches on the rocks and drifted to the mouth of the cave. A stiff wind was blowing from the east and whipping the coconut fronds into tangles. The surf was up and washing across the sand to the trees lining the beach. The two drifted up to perch on the rocks on the clifftop.

"We could have done some roaming before coming here. We could have stopped by the town hall. It'sth the lasth night of the play."

He turned to look at her. "Don't complain. You've seen it so many times you know the bolom's lines by heart."

"Yeth, that part was written for me. Funny thing is he doesn't give it a name. He justh calls it bolom."

"It was never born. It never saw the light of day."

"Oh! Didn't you see the end? It got life when he said *'Stretch your wings and soar, pass over the fields / Like the salt shadow of night . . .'* So it soars to the edge of light – it getsth life and it goes off with the hero who becometh his brother. If I got life I'd soar, I'd dance all the way to the light."

She slipped off her rock and perched on the grass at the base of the rock on which he crouched.

"Did you ever think of the name you would have if you were born? What did they call you in your imagined life?"

"Nothing. I didn't have a name."

"A name is important. I'm sure no one can go into the light without a name."

"I hadn't thought about it. I was concentrating on creating a happy family." He was silent for a while. He sighed and turned to look at her. "Joshua, I guess. That's the name that comes to mind. I would have been Joshua and they would call me Josh for short. Did you have a name?"

"I named myself Marianne. It'sth the sort of name I think my mother would have called me. I would have been Marianne, accomplished actress and dancer." She paused, then floated up to sit beside him on the rock. "I like Josh. The name suits you. Now we know our names, let'sth use them." She turned to face him directly. "From now on I'll call you Josh and you musth call me Marianne."

He nodded.

"It's so blustery it would be strange if anyone showed up to walk on the beach," she said. "Let'sth go roaming. There'sth so much to explore."

"I'm staying right here." He turned his back to her. "As long as there's a chance she'll come along, I'll wait."

The wind had subsided but the sea was still choppy with some high waves washing across the beach.

"Here she comes, Marianne."

She sat up and looked towards the bay. "I don't see anyone."

"She's there; standing next to that tree near the middle of the beach."

"Oh, yesth, I see." Marianne put her hand over her eyes and spotted the figure leaning against the trunk of one of the coconut trees. She didn't seem to mind the waves that washed up to the stand of trees. "She'sth getting soaked. Why is she out here in thisth weather?"

"I don't know." Josh leaned forward and kept looking intently at the figure. "I've never seen her on the beach in bad weather like this. Look how she's leaning her head against the tree and holding on. I've never seen her do that before." They both leaned forward, watching the shadowy figure who was pressing her forehead against the tree trunk.

They waited for a long while, then he floated to the edge of the cliff. Marianne followed. The woman hadn't moved. Marianne turned to Josh.

"Is she going to stay there forever?"

"I don't know. Something must be wrong."

"Like what? The storm?" Marianne glanced at him and then back at the woman. "Looksth like she has a silent storm inside her."

Josh didn't say anything but kept looking at the woman. After a while he turned to look at the horizon.

"It will soon be dawn. There are clouds but they'll blow over. We'll have to leave before the sun comes out."

"Look, Josh, she'sth leaving the tree. See? She'sth beginning to walk along the beach."

"Strange, she's walking towards the water. Let's go closer."

They glided from the clifftop to the beach. The woman's clothes were soaked and her long skirt clung to her legs, making it difficult for her to walk. She staggered into the water, her legs pushing against the surf.

"Marianne, she can't possibly be thinking of bathing in that sea!"

"No, Josh. She'sth walking with a purpose, just like my mother did. I couldn't stop her but perhapth the two of uths can do something to stop your mother."

"Like what? What can we do?"

"We can ride the crests of the waveths and push her back."

They skipped to the water and hovered above the waves that galloped towards the shore. The woman pushed against the waves. She stumbled as her skirts caught and tangled around her legs. She suddenly disappeared where the sea floor sloped sharply down. Her head appeared above the surface and her arms flailed as she coughed and struggled to breathe.

"Let'sth push her back, Josh. We mustn't let the undertow pull her in."

As another wave gathered and rushed in, Marianne threw herself against the woman as she surfaced again, gasping. Josh rode the crest of the next wave and slammed against her before she disappeared again under the water. They kept doing this until the force of the waves and their pushing had her rolling in the sandy wash on the beach.

Marianne and Josh hovered at the water's edge while the woman coughed and retched as she tried to rise on her hands and knees. It was getting light. An orange glow spread across the horizon as the dark clouds drifted towards the west. Marianne and Josh were busy observing the woman and they didn't pay attention to the changing light.

"We did it, Josh, we did it. Your mother'ths safe."

"Yes, she is. I want to take a closer look." He drifted over to where she was bent over on her hands and knees, trying to get rid of the water she had swallowed and breathed in. He floated around her, then hovered over her back.

Marianne called out to him. "Come on, Josh. See? The sun'ths already coming up above the horizon. If we don't go now she'll wonder at the two rotting lumpths of flesh on the beach. That'sth all that will be left of us."

Josh turned. The sun was casting a swath of golden light on the water which was now calmer.

"It's up already, Marianne, and nothing's happened. See? Look at you! You're shining, like light, and I can see all of you; your face and hands and feet."

Marianne stretched out her arms.

"I can see you too, Josh. My, you're so good looking! We saved your mother and I think somehow we're free! We're free, Josh. No clumpths of flesh, no puny selves. All free, all spirith, all light!" They floated in circles above her, drifted towards the surf and soared above the waves dancing in the path of sunlight on the water.

The woman sat on the sand, pushed her hair from her face and dusted sand from her arms and clothes. She wrung water from her skirt and looked out to sea. It was calmer now than it had been when she had decided to walk into it. She felt lighter than she had then, lighter than when she had dashed out into the storm. She felt as though a weight had been lifted from her. The sun was up and it cast a warm golden glow over the bay.

The sea had rejected her, had coughed her up when she had gone under and known she wouldn't have a chance to save herself. The force of it had been absolute. Now she knew for certain she was meant to carry on.

She looked out over the water towards the horizon and saw what at first appeared to be two birds flying low over the surface of the sea towards the sun. They were larger than the birds she'd seen before and as they moved she noticed they were different in shape. They dipped and swirled, wings extended towards the sun. As she continued to watch they began to soar. What she thought were wing tips were hands that reached out to clasp each other. They moved, twirling in patterned steps, silhouettes etched in sunlight, dancing towards the rim of the sea.

She felt light and free. She got up, smiled, turned and walked purposefully towards the village.

Tapestry

Felice sat hunched over her embroidery hoop, her glasses perched on the tip of her nose. She looked up occasionally over the rim to check a paper pattern that was spread on the table in front of her. A length of aida cloth with colourful images hung from one side of the hoop. Every once in a while she set the hoop on the table, spread the cloth out, her head tilted to one side as she surveyed the work. Then she picked up the hoop again and continued to work. Her hands moved quickly as she thrust the needle through one hole of a square of the aida cloth, pulled it up through the top part of the hoop and thrust it down diagonally through another hole to make a series of crosses and shape the stitches into the pattern she was creating. It was the image of a young woman, smiling, in graduation robes, the mortar board askew on her head and her arm raised, holding a scroll. Her feet and shoes were hidden by a flowering shrub which Felice was now working on. She wanted to complete that section of the cloth before her granddaughter arrived later. It was her way of showing her that she was proud of her.

When she began working the cloth she had intended it to be a runner for her dining table but she realized from the scenes and characters she had included it was inappropriate for that purpose. It was more like a tapestry, depicting scenes from her environment and events from her life. She had included them on a whim based on whatever her memory had tossed up as she worked. Now that she looked at them she discovered that they were in some sort of chronological order with events from her childhood first.

She looked up over the rim of her glasses as Adele, her caregiver, entered the room. Adele shook her head and gave Felice a disapproving look.

"You know you should be resting now. I didn' come before because I thought you were sleeping but I see I have to check on you more. How you get the work basket?"

Felice smiled. "I went over there and got it."

"Now suppose you had fall down? How you think I could explain that, eh?"

"Adele, I'm not an invalid. You worry too much. If I don't move around I won't be able to get up at all after a while. I'm okay."

"So you been working all this time on this fine fine stitching you doing. What about your eyes, eh? And later you going ask me to rub your hands. You not so young now, you know. You overdoing things and I will get the blame."

"Don't be silly. Look! You like it? I finish the part with Eva so I can show her later. You like it?"

"It beautiful, oui! Yes, it really nice. All these small stitches and the colours. I don't know how you doing all this."

"My eyes and hands are still good and as long as they good, I'll keep stitching. You think Eva will like it?"

"How you mean? She must like it, oui. Is for her you doing it, yes?"

"Yes. She's the only one I have left. It has many stories, some secrets. I'll have to tell her. Maybe Eva can keep a secret."

You soon run out of cloth, you know. Now you finish the part with Miss Eva what you going to put in this last part? I see you start it already."

"That's a secret. You and Eva will find out when it's finished."

Adele started to put the floss into the work basket. "You need to put it away now, Miss Felice. You must get a rest before Miss Eva come. Here, let me fold this for you. Relax now, I'll bring your tea and medicine. You have time for a little rest."

"Thanks, Adele, but I don't want to be drowsy. Let's leave the medicine for later."

Adele opened her mouth and pointed with her index finger as though she was about to reprimand Felice. She shook her head, picked up the work basket and put it in the centre of the table, out of Felice's reach.

"As long as I don't get blame if something happen to you. Rest a little and I'll bring the tea."

"Let's leave the tea too, till Eva comes. We'll have so much to talk about."

Adele shook her head again and walked to the door. Felice smiled and looked at her as she walked away. As soon as Adele shut the door, she got up, shuffled around the table and pushed the work basket towards the end where she was sitting. She hummed a tune as she opened it and began taking out the needlework.

Eva pulled her chair closer to her grandmother's. Felice looked at her with a worried expression.

"I hope Martha doesn't mind you're going to stay with me for the rest of your vacation."

"Oh no, she doesn't. I already spent two weeks with her. Besides, she has other grandchildren and I'm the only one you have."

"True. But I always remember how fussy she was when Denis and your mother had to live here for a few months after they got married; before they got their own place. But a lot of time has passed so I suppose it's okay now."

"I'm sure it is, Nanfie, and I'm looking forward to spending this time with you. Remember? You promised to teach me how to cross-stitch so here's your chance. I'll be gone for quite a while when I go back to study."

Felice leaned back in her chair and smiled.

"I so proud of you, Eva. Imagine my only grandchile a doctor. Your father would be proud of you too."

"I know. But I think he'd be proud of me whatever career I chose."

"That's true. I wish he was here and your mother too."

"Me too. I miss both of them."

"The laws for drunk driving not strict enough. The person who slammed right into their car and killed them still alive and my only son and his wife gone. Life too hard."

"It hurts to think about it, Nanfie, but I'm sure they'd want us to remember the good times and the good things that have happened since. You and Grandma Martha are closer now, aren't you? And they did change the law."

"Yes, but it still not strict enough. Look! I stitched a pattern of them on their wedding day." She reached into her basket, pulled out the cloth and put it on the table.

Eva stood up and helped to spread it out.

"It's lovely, Nanfie. So many images and so colourful. Yes, this part looks like Mama and Pa. How did you get it done?"

"You remember the website for creating patterns you told me about? I couldn't work that out. Too old for all that but they had a mailing address so I sent the photographs I wanted designed and they sent back the patterns with suggestions for the colours of the floss. It didn't cost much either. All these other images I made up the patterns for them myself. See here? Look at this one of you on graduation day."

"Oh yes! It does look like me too. Even the dress I was wearing. And that other one looks just like Mama and Pa! You're really good at this, Nanfie. It's lovely."

"I hoped you would like it because I'm going to give it to you. I'm working on the last part while you're here so you can learn how to stitch using the counted method. You can work on something of your own too."

"Okay, I'll sit with you for an hour or so when you're working so I can learn. What about all these other scenes?"

"Most of them are from my life; things that happened, mostly."

"What about this one? That's an image of the Virgin Mary, isn't it?"

"Yes, and these little girls are flower girls. When I was small my mother used to send me to be a flower girl in the procession. We had baskets of petals and we used to throw them in front of the statue which older girls used to carry on a pallet on their shoulders. See? I put in two flower girls. I don't think they do processions like that anymore."

"I don't remember them so they must have stopped. What about these two figures? This one is surrounded by dark shadows. How come?"

"His story not nice. I never told anyone, but since the cloth will be yours, I'll tell you."

Eva sat down while Felice folded the cloth, leaving the image with the two figures exposed.

"I was about ten at the time, preparing for confirmation. It was my first year in secondary school too. The nuns used to make us observe all the feasts as a school group. Once a month, every first Thursday, they would take all of us, the Catholics, that is, to the church for confession and then to the first Friday mass on the next day. Several priests would come to hear the confessions so we could get back to school by midday. This one in the sunshine is Father Benedict. I liked going to him for confession. He always told me a story that helped me to understand why it was important to avoid certain things. He was our chaplain and popular with everybody. He would come to the school to lead the retreats during Lent. See? He's in the sunshine. He used to stand in the sun and we used to say he wanted to get brown like us." She chuckled.

"This other one, Père Auguste, was different. He had problems and he could hardly speak English at first. The first time I went to him for confession he asked me if I had pwèl. Can you imagine? I was shocked. I couldn't say anything. I knelt there with my head down. He went on for a while asking foolish questions. Did my sister have pwèl? Did I see it? What was it like? I didn't have a sister and I didn't bother to answer. I wouldn't answer him anyway, even if I had a sister. After a while he stopped talking but I could hear him breathing through the lattice that separated the compartments. Then he said, 'Pardon, sorry. Allez. You ave to go. Stand up and I will give you absolution.'

"Mind you, he was the one who had done all the talking and I hadn't confessed anything. I stood up because I wanted to get out of there fast. I could see through the lattice and I couldn't believe what I saw. He had exposed himself and was holding on to his penis. I ran out and went to the pews where we had to sit when we were finished with confession. I looked around but no one else seemed to be upset. I knew I was not the first or the only girl who had gone to that confessional but no one seemed to be distracted. I leaned back against the seat of the pew looking around, then I felt a hard slap on my back which pitched me forward. I heard the principal's voice saying 'Sit up and don't slouch.' She hit so hard I almost swallowed my tongue.

"I didn't tell anyone about this. I couldn't. I thought if he had done this to other girls they would have said something and the bishop would have sent him away but he stayed and was in that same confessional for years. I tried to avoid him by going to the section where Father Benedict was but I couldn't always manage it. I would let others take my turn and then I would go to the after-confession pews sometimes without having gone to confession. That way I avoided him but I also missed confession and I would worry because I would have to go to communion without having confessed. I thought I was done for, thought it was all my fault; that I had done something wrong to make him say the things he said and behave in the way he did. It had to be my fault because no one else seemed upset.

"A few times I got away with pretending to be sick on the first Thursday so I wouldn't have to go to school. Why didn't I tell my mother? I thought she wouldn't believe me. I couldn't tell the nuns either because if they were so quick to slap our backs for what they called slouching I was sure they wouldn't want to hear anything like that. I wouldn't know how to approach them anyway. So I kept it all to myself and I avoided him as much as I could. I had almost forgotten about this but the recent news about the scandals in the church brought it all back. I should have said something at the time but I didn't and I thought perhaps that by not speaking up others may have had to go through what I did. That's why I stitched this. To recognize Father Benedict's goodness with this bright yellow and the flowers. This was also my small way of showing up Père Auguste. That's why he's in shadow and has a leering look. It sets him apart from Father Benedict. Do you notice the difference? It's my way of getting a little revenge."

"Yes. It's striking, Nanfie. The brilliant yellow and lighter colours contrast with the dark grey and sepia hues. The colours say something about the characters."

Felice leaned back in her chair and closed her eyes. Eva went and sat on the arm of her chair. She reached out and took Felice's hand.

"Are you okay, Nanfie? You look a little pale."

Felice opened her eyes, sighed and closed them again.

"It's the palpitations." She put her free hand over her heart. "Telling you about this upset me all over again. Just think of how many might have been hurt because of Père Auguste. I should have said something."

"Nanfie, you were only ten. You shouldn't blame yourself. There were probably other victims like you. You must forget it now. Did Miss Adele give you your medicine? You know you must take it every day. Did you?"

Felice pointed to a side table with a small tray and a glass of water. "It's over there."

Eva went across to the table to get the pills. By the time she went back, Felice had drifted off to sleep.

"Look at this, Nanfie. What do you think?"

Felice took the square of aida cloth that Eva gave her.

"You getting good at this, Miss Eva. You preparing for the neat stitching you have to do on bodies when you become a surgeon."

Eva smiled. "I'm not even sure what I want to specialize in yet. But this stitching is relaxing. It will calm me when I get stressed."

"Stressed my foot." Felice sucked her teeth, making a loud sound. "If you take after your grandpa, you ain't going get stress."

Eva giggled. "If I take after Grandma Martha, I'll definitely get stressed. If she were here, she'd be frowning and tut tutting because you steupsed just now, sucking your teeth. If I did that, she would say 'Stop it! That's rude!'" They laughed.

"Not even someone like Martha could make Lionel feel stress. He was laid back, cool you'd say. And he liked to dance. That's how we met. I went to this party and he asked me to dance and we ended up dancing together the whole night. After that he was my best dancing partner and then we became life partners. After I met him no one else could interest me. We had a good life but he died too young. Denis was only five. Lionel liked fishing as much as he liked dancing. Spear fishing. I used to go with him to the beach and wait while he went diving and spear fishing. After Denis was born I couldn't go as often and I was at home on the day he didn't come back. It was cloudy that day and I don't like the beach on cloudy days. I asked him not to go but he said it was snapper season and he wanted to catch a few. It's my favourite and Lionel always tried to get them for me. He usually came home by six so he could spend time with Denis and then with me, in the evening, together.

"I knew something was wrong when he didn't come home. I called his fishing partner, Ralph, but he said he hadn't gone because he had the flu and the weather hadn't been good. He went out to the beach where they usually fished and he called me to say there was no sign of Lionel but he found his clothes and slippers under the sea grape tree where they usually left their things. Ralph said he had alerted the coast guard right away but I knew that something bad had happened.

"I dressed Denis early next morning and went to the beach. Ralph was already there. A coast guard boat was out on the water a short distance from the shore and two divers were looking for him. When they brought him up he was still clutching his spear and he looked just as if he was coming in from a swim except that a fish or something had nibbled his upper lip and there was a raw white spot of flesh.

"Up to today I'm still not sure what happened. He was a good swimmer. The autopsy report said he drowned but something must have happened to cause that. I don't know if they checked everything. I worried about it until one night I dreamt that we were at the beach and he came out of the sea all wet and smiling. He knelt in the sand in front of me and Denis and he said, 'I'm okay, don't worry.' He picked Denis up and lifted him high in the air as he used to do. I woke up crying. See? I stitched this scene here – Denis laughing while Lionel lifts him high in the air. The dream seemed so real; but I had to carry on and raise Denis on my own. He grew up to be a good man, like his father. I miss both of them. Sometimes you only realize how deeply you love after the loved one is gone."

Eva sat on a chair close to the bed. Felice slept fitfully and she opened her eyes occasionally and muttered. Eva could only make out some words if she bent close to Felice. There were moments when Felice was lucid and had snatches of conversation but these were few.

Adele came into the room and handed Eva a cup of tea.

"How she doing, Miss Eva?"

"So, so, Miss Adele. Sometimes she's wide awake and we talk, but she drifts off and talks about all sorts of things. Most times I don't know what she's talking about but I know her mind must be on Grandpa because she says his name often."

"She travelling, Miss Eva. That's what they call travelling. The old people say when somebody dying their spirit does travel and they seeing all sort of thing that happen in their life and other things too."

"She has trouble breathing so sometimes it's hard to make out what she says."

"I don understand how she take a turn so sudden."

"The doctor said it's the heart causing fluid to build up in her chest and her lungs. Best we can do is make sure we give her the medication and keep her comfortable. She's a little brighter today."

"Like she was waiting for you to come."

"I wish we had more time together. The month went by so quickly. I was enjoying my time with her."

"Before you come, Miss Felice push herself too hard with all that stitching. I tell she so but she didn't listen. Like she know she didn have much time and she did want to finish the cloth she give you."

Eva handed the teacup to Adele.

"Thanks for the tea. Maybe we can get Nanfie to drink a little broth today. You can make some light chicken broth for her?"

"Yes, I start to make it already. Call me when you ready."

"Thanks, Miss Adele."

Felice opened her eyes and looked at Eva who reached out and held her hand. She motioned to Adele who helped her lift Felice into a sitting position. They puffed up her pillows and propped her back against them.

"I'll bring the soup quick, Miss Eva." Adele hurried out of the room.

"Lionel was here. He brought some snapper for supper. Did you see him?"

"No, Nanfie. You must have been dreaming."

"No, no. He was here. Saw him clear as day."

"Have a sip of water." Eva put a straw into her grandmother's mouth and held the glass as she sipped.

"Enough . . . what's today?"

"Thursday, Nanfie. You got sick on Tuesday. Doctor says you must rest to avoid getting palpitations."

"The old heart tired, Eva . . ."

They sat quietly for a while. Felice closed her eyes. Eva pulled the blanket up under her chin and tucked her arm under it. Felice turned her head to look at Eva.

"Thursday . . . today is confession. . . . If is Père Auguste I not going . . ." Her voice trailed off. She closed her eyes. After a while she spoke softly with her eyes closed. "I didn't tell you all the story . . ." Her voice trailed off again and Eva leaned closer to hear her. She spoke in snatches with pauses in between as she seemed to drift into deep thought. "Didn't tell you how he opened the lattice . . . when I stood up . . . he grabbed my hand and made me touch him . . . touched me too, all over . . . felt dirty . . . I ran when he let go my hand."

"You must let this go now, Nanfie. Wasn't your fault." Eva patted her grandmother's hand.

"Couldn't confess that . . . lost faith . . . lost all . . . Call Father Benedict . . ."

"He's not here, Nanfie. He died a long time ago. Both of them. Try to forget. Do you want me to call Father John? He's kind and understanding. I can ask him to hear your confession and give you a blessing with the holy oils. May I?"

There was a long silence, then Felice looked at Eva and nodded.

While Adele fed Felice some broth, Eva went to arrange for the priest to visit. He went back with her to the house.

"I'll speak with her for a while to hear her confession and you can come in when I do the anointing and blessing."

She sat outside the door while he went in, holding a small vial of oil. Eva witnessed her grandmother receiving the last rites and she sat at her bedside after Father John left. Felice seemed more peaceful. She had drifted off to sleep but her breathing was shallow. It was getting dark outside. Eva turned on the bedside lamp.

Felice opened her eyes.

"Is late, but Lionel coming. See him down the street?"

Eva got up to close the window and draw the curtains. She went back to sit beside the bed and she pulled up the blanket to tuck it over her grandmother's shoulders. Felice gave a deep sigh and was quiet.

Eva and her grandmother walked slowly, stopping to examine each exhibit.

"How did you manage this?" Martha turned to look at Eva. "I never knew Felice had done so much work."

"I asked the people I knew she had given samplers as gifts and they were happy to loan them when I explained I wanted to exhibit her work."

"Impressive, I must say!" Martha stepped back, her back tilted at a slight angle, her grey hair in layered curls around her head. She removed her glasses, shut one eye and looked through one of the lenses with the other. She put the glasses back on, leaned forward, squinted, then stood upright. "This is really remarkable, Eva. Why didn't she do anything with all this before?"

"She was happy working them and giving them away as birthday and anniversary gifts."

"Hmph!" Martha clicked her tongue.

Eva glanced at her quickly.

"It's a pity you two didn't get to know each other better, Grandma. I'm sure you would have enjoyed her company and she would have created something special for you."

"Hmm. I don't know. Felice Fevrier kept to herself. Anyway, we always moved in different circles. I sometimes wondered whether she had any social circle at all. She worked a piece she gave your parents for their wedding. The two hands holding white doves. Did you find it in the trunk?"

"Yes, it's over there." They walked along and stopped in front of another exhibit. "See? Fresh and perfect as though she stitched it yesterday."

They looked at the piece with a hand of the groom and bride each holding a white dove, the names Maria and Denis with the date of the wedding stitched in below.

"That belonged to your parents so it's yours now," Martha said.

"Can you keep it for me while I'm away? It would look good on the wall where you have the family pictures. I have a large piece she gave me and I want to take it with me. I can't take both. Let me show you the other piece. It's the main attraction of the exhibition."

They walked across the room and stopped in front of the wall which was covered almost from one end to the other with an elaborate sampler.

"This is the one she gave me."

"A tapestry. So detailed . . ."

"And colourful. Isn't it exquisite? This is me on graduation day." Eva pointed to the image of herself in robes, holding a scroll aloft.

"This one looks like your parents on their wedding day. Who would have thought? How did she do this?"

"Nanfie was gifted, Grandma."

"This looks like two priests who were in our parish a long time ago. That's Father Benedict for sure and this one . . . this must be Père Auguste." She chuckled. "We used to call him Père Perv. He shouldn't have been a priest at all. He was closer to a pervert. We used to avoid him and laugh at the things he used to say."

"Didn't you or anyone ever report him?"

"Ha! Who would we have reported him to? And who would have listened? They wouldn't have believed us anyhow. All of them were considered beyond reproach. We just made fun of it. Felice must have known something because the contrast between the two images is stark. They sent him away eventually and that was good. He wasn't around by the time we got to sixth form. This last bit is fascinating. Looks like Felice herself walking away and waving goodbye."

"Yes, it is. This is how she captured her death. She's smiling so she must have been happy to go. I think of Nanfie and Grandpa together somewhere, dancing and happy."

Acknowledgements

Thanks to colleagues at Writers' Ink Inc. for encouragement and helpful critiques. Special thanks to Esther Phillips, Linda Deane, Edison Williams, Christine Barrow, Harclyde Walcott and Robert Edison Sandiford. Much appreciation to Antonia MacDonald for constructive comments and to Shivaun Hearne and the editorial team at the University of the West Indies Press for their careful reading of the manuscript and valuable feedback. To my family for generous support and to Kath for the cover image – mèsi boku.